Dangerous Pleasures

Summeer Fox

Published by Summeer Fox, 2024.

DANGEROUS PLEASURES

First edition. September 14, 2024.

Copyright © 2024 Summeer Fox.

ISBN: 979-8227974594

Written by Summeer Fox.

Table of Contents

Chapter 1: The Unfamiliar Hunger

*M*ae had always known the smell of earth. It clung to her skin like a second layer, even here, in a world far from the fields and barns she had left behind. The university hallways were filled with the sharp scent of new paper, overheated radiators, and the artificial sweetness of city perfumes. Yet, Mae carried the farm with her — the sun-baked clay under her nails, the scent of hay lingering in her hair. She felt out of place among the polished shoes and soft, uncalloused hands.

She sat in the back of the literature lecture hall, trying to disappear into her seat. Her boots, scuffed and sturdy, were tucked beneath her chair, her fingers tapping nervously on the edge of her notebook. Her eyes, however, were not on the pages. They were on him.

Professor Arden was everything the city promised — tall, composed, with a voice like dark molasses that poured smoothly over the room. His eyes, sharp and intelligent, moved across the faces of his students as he spoke. He had an air of confidence that seemed effortless, a presence that demanded attention without ever raising his voice.

Mae watched his mouth form the words, her focus drawn to the way his lips moved, the slight curve at the corners when he made a point he found particularly clever. She felt an unfamiliar stirring inside her, a low hum in her veins, something both thrilling and unsettling.

His gaze landed on her more than once, lingering a moment too long. Each time, she felt a jolt, a flicker of recognition, as if he could see past her rough edges, her awkwardness, straight into the parts of her she kept hidden — even from herself.

After class, she lingered near the door, pretending to fumble with her bag. She wanted to hear his voice again, feel that flicker of attention. As the students filtered out, he approached, his steps unhurried.

"Mae, isn't it?" His voice was softer, more personal than when he lectured.

Her heart leapt at the sound of her name on his lips. "Yes, sir," she managed, hoping she sounded steadier than she felt.

"I noticed you in the back," he said, his eyes appraising. "Are you understanding the material?"

She nodded quickly, too quickly. "I think so," she lied. In truth, the texts felt like they were written in another language, the poetry dense and elusive.

He smiled, a knowing smile, and stepped closer. "If you ever need help, don't hesitate to ask. My office hours are open... or if you'd prefer, we could arrange a time more convenient for you."

The offer hung in the air, heavy with implication. Her breath caught. "Thank you," she whispered, feeling a blush creep up her neck. "I might do that."

His gaze held hers, unblinking, and for a moment, the world outside the small bubble they created seemed to fall away. "Good," he murmured, his voice low. "I hope you do."

Mae nodded, unsure what else to say. She felt exposed under his gaze, like he could see everything she was thinking. She swallowed hard, and then he stepped back, breaking the connection. She felt both relief and an odd sense of loss as he turned back to his desk.

She walked out of the lecture hall, her steps brisk, her mind racing. The air outside was cool against her flushed skin. She inhaled deeply, trying to calm the flutter in her chest. But all she could think about was the way he had looked at her, the heat in his eyes, the way his voice had dipped when he spoke her name.

That night, as Mae lay in her narrow dorm bed, she found her thoughts circling back to him. She closed her eyes, but his image was there, behind her eyelids — the dark eyes, the knowing smile, the way his fingers had brushed ever so lightly against hers when he handed her a book.

She felt a pull, a deep, magnetic draw that she didn't quite understand, a craving that had nothing to do with hunger or thirst, something more primal, more profound. Her fingers brushed her own lips, imagining the feel of his, the warmth of his breath on her skin.

Mae had never felt anything like this before — this deep, twisting need, this ache that settled low in her belly. She pressed her thighs together, trying to ignore it, trying to push the thought of him away, but it was useless. He was there, in her mind, in her body, in the spaces between breaths.

The next morning, she found herself at his office door, her heart pounding, her palms damp with nerves. She knocked softly, and the door opened almost immediately.

He stood there, his eyes dark and curious, a faint smile playing at the corners of his mouth. "Mae," he said, a hint of surprise in his voice, though his gaze suggested he had been expecting her all along. "Come in."

She stepped inside, the door closing behind her with a soft click, and she knew, in that moment, that whatever this was, whatever had begun between them, it was far from over.

Chapter 2: A Meeting of Minds and Flesh

Mae sat in the dimly lit office, feeling the thrum of her heartbeat in her ears. Professor Arden stood just a few feet away, leaning against his desk, arms crossed over his chest. His expression was unreadable, his dark eyes fixed on her with a curiosity that felt almost predatory. She could still feel the lingering heat of his hand from where he had touched her shoulder moments before.

"So," he began, his voice low and deliberate, "what brings you here, Mae?"

Her throat felt tight, her mouth suddenly dry. She swallowed, trying to find her voice. "I... I needed help with the reading," she managed, her voice a bit too high, too rushed.

He nodded, his gaze never leaving her face. "Is that all?"

She hesitated, knowing there was more she wanted to say, more she wanted to ask, but unsure of how to put it into words. The air between them felt thick, charged with something unspoken. "No," she admitted finally, "that's not all."

He smiled, just a hint of it, as if he'd been expecting this answer. "Good," he murmured, pushing away from the desk and moving closer. "Because I don't think either of us came here just to talk about books."

Her breath caught in her throat, and she felt a flush spread across her cheeks. He was standing so close now, close enough that she could feel the warmth radiating from his body, could catch the faint scent of cedar and something deeper, more intoxicating.

"I don't know what you mean," she whispered, though she knew exactly what he meant.

He tilted his head, his gaze never wavering. "Don't you?" he asked softly, his voice a velvet caress that sent a shiver down her spine. "Because I think you do."

Her body betrayed her, leaning in ever so slightly, her breath catching. "Maybe," she whispered, the word a confession.

He reached out, his fingers lightly brushing her forearm, trailing up toward her shoulder. "You intrigue me, Mae," he said, his touch sending sparks along her skin. "You're different from the others... there's something about you that I can't quite figure out."

She felt her pulse quicken at his words, a mixture of fear and excitement coursing through her veins. "Is that a good thing?" she asked, her voice barely above a whisper.

His smile widened, a slow, sensual curve that made her insides twist. "I think so," he replied, his hand moving to cup her chin, his thumb brushing lightly over her bottom lip. "I think I'd like to find out just how different you are."

Mae's breath came faster, her mind racing. She should step back, she should leave, but his touch was like a magnet, pulling her closer, drawing her into him. "I... I don't know if this is a good idea," she whispered, but even to her own ears, her words lacked conviction.

He leaned in, his lips a whisper away from hers, his breath warm against her skin. "Maybe not," he agreed, his voice low and husky, "but I think it's an idea neither of us can ignore."

She closed her eyes, feeling the tension coil tighter within her. She felt his lips brush against hers, soft at first, a testing caress, as if waiting for her to pull away. When she didn't, he deepened the kiss, his mouth claiming hers, firm and confident. She felt a jolt, a spark of electricity shooting through her, igniting something deep within.

Mae's hands found his shoulders, her fingers digging into the fabric of his shirt, her body pressing closer of its own accord. His kiss was demanding, and she responded, her lips parting under his, her breath mingling with his as their mouths moved together in a dance of need and hunger.

His hands moved down her back, pulling her against him, and she felt the hard lines of his body through the thin fabric of her blouse. She moaned softly, the sound swallowed by his mouth, and felt his grip tighten, his hands roaming, exploring. He pushed her back against the wall, his body pressing into hers, firm and unyielding.

"Do you want this?" he murmured against her lips, his breath hot, his hands sliding up her sides.

"Yes," she breathed, her voice shaky but certain. "I want this."

He smiled against her mouth, a sound that was more a low growl than anything else. "Good," he murmured, his hands moving to her waist, lifting her slightly, his body pressing her against the wall. "Because I've been wanting this since the first moment I saw you."

She gasped, her hands clutching his shoulders, her legs wrapping around his waist instinctively. She could feel the heat of him through their clothes, the hardness of his desire pressing against her core. Her body arched toward him, a soft moan escaping her lips as his mouth moved to her neck, his teeth grazing her skin, sending shivers racing down her spine.

His hands slid under her blouse, fingers tracing the curve of her spine, his touch firm, insistent. "You're beautiful," he whispered against her skin, his lips moving lower, kissing the hollow of her throat, the curve of her shoulder.

She could barely breathe, her body tingling with sensation, her mind spinning with the intensity of it all. "Michael," she gasped, his name slipping out before she could stop it.

He froze for a moment, then pulled back slightly, his eyes dark with desire. "Say it again," he commanded softly, his hands tightening on her hips.

"Michael," she repeated, her voice a soft plea.

He groaned, his lips finding hers again in a fierce kiss, his hands moving with purpose, exploring, claiming her as his. She felt herself surrendering to him, to the sensations coursing through her, her body arching against his, needing more, wanting everything.

His hands found the hem of her skirt, sliding it up, his fingers grazing the soft skin of her thigh. "Tell me to stop," he whispered against her lips, but there was no hesitation in his movements, no uncertainty in his touch.

She shook her head, her fingers tangling in his hair, pulling him closer. "Don't stop," she whispered, her voice breathless, desperate. "Don't ever stop."

He smiled, a wicked grin that sent a thrill through her, his hands moving higher, finding the edge of her panties, tugging them down, his fingers sliding between her thighs, finding her wet and ready. "Good girl," he murmured, his voice thick with satisfaction, his lips brushing against her ear. "Let me show you how good this can be."

She gasped as his fingers found her center, stroking her gently at first, teasing, and then harder, more insistent. Her body *responded instantly, a wave of pleasure crashing over her, her hips rocking against his hand, her breath coming in short, sharp pants.*

"That's it," he whispered, his voice a low growl, his fingers moving faster, his mouth capturing hers in a fierce, possessive kiss. "Let go for me, Mae. Let go."

And she did, her body shuddering, her breath catching in her throat as she tumbled over the edge, her hands clutching his shoulders, her lips parting in a silent cry. He held her as she came apart in his arms, his touch never wavering, his mouth moving against hers, coaxing, guiding, until she was spent, her body trembling in the aftermath.

He pulled back slightly, his eyes softening as he looked at her, a smile playing at his lips. "You're incredible," he murmured, his fingers still tracing lazy circles against her skin.

She blinked, trying to steady her breath, her heart still racing. "So are you," she whispered, her voice a mix of awe and desire.

He chuckled softly, his hands moving to cup her face, his thumbs brushing against her cheeks. "This is just the beginning," he promised, his voice a low rumble that sent another shiver down her spine. "I want more of you, Mae. Much more."

And as he kissed her again, slow and deep, she knew that she wanted more too. Much more.

Chapter 3: The Edge of Exposure

The days seemed longer now, each moment stretching thin with anticipation. Mae moved through her classes in a haze, her thoughts constantly drifting back to Michael — the way his hands had moved over her skin, the taste of his kiss, the hunger in his eyes. She felt like she was on the brink of something, teetering between exhilaration and fear, desire and caution.

In class, she could feel his gaze on her, subtle but intense, like a steady flame that flickered and danced just for her. Each look felt like a secret, a touch without touching. She found herself craving his attention, longing for the next time they could be alone. But beneath the thrill was a gnawing unease — a whisper of doubt that grew louder with each passing day.

After a week of stolen glances and whispered words, Michael asked her to meet him again. This time, it was not in his office, but in a small, tucked-away cafe on the edge of campus. The choice felt safer, more discreet, but still risky. She felt her pulse quicken as she approached the door, the bell above it chiming softly as she stepped inside.

He was already there, seated at a corner table, a cup of coffee in front of him, his posture relaxed but alert. When he saw her, he smiled, a slow, deliberate curve of his lips that sent a shiver through her. "Mae," he greeted, standing as she approached. "I'm glad you came."

"I couldn't stay away," she admitted, a nervous laugh escaping her lips. She took the seat across from him, her hands folding in her lap to hide the slight tremor in her fingers.

He leaned forward, his eyes never leaving hers. "Good," he murmured. "I was afraid you might have changed your mind."

She shook her head, a small smile playing at her lips. "No, I haven't changed my mind." But her heart was beating a little too fast, and she felt a flush creeping up her neck. "But I am a little... nervous."

Michael reached across the table, his fingers brushing against hers, a light touch that sent warmth spreading through her hand. "There's nothing to be nervous about," he reassured her, his voice low and soothing. "We're just two people having coffee."

"Two people who shouldn't be doing this," she added quietly, glancing around the room, suddenly aware of how exposed they were, even in this secluded spot.

He smiled, his fingers tightening around hers for a moment before pulling back. "If it makes you uncomfortable, we don't have to meet like this," he said, his tone sincere. "I don't want you to feel pressured, Mae. You're in control of this."

She took a deep breath, calming the flutter in her chest. "I know," she replied softly. "But I want to be here. I just... don't want anyone to find out."

His expression grew serious, his eyes darkening with concern. "We'll be careful," he promised. "But we can't let fear stop us from exploring this... whatever it is."

Mae nodded, feeling a mixture of relief and excitement at his words. "Whatever it is," she echoed, her voice steadying. "I'm not ready to let it go."

He smiled again, his eyes softening. "Neither am I." He paused, then added, "I want you to know that I think about you... all the time."

Her breath caught in her throat, and she felt a thrill run through her. "I think about you too," she confessed, her cheeks warming under his gaze.

They talked for a while longer, their conversation flowing with ease. But there was always an undercurrent, a tension that simmered just below the surface, a silent acknowledgment of what lay between them. She could feel his eyes on her, feel the weight of his desire, and it made her pulse quicken, her breath shallow.

As they finished their drinks, Michael glanced at his watch, a small frown creasing his brow. "I have a meeting soon," he said reluctantly, "but I don't want this to end."

"Neither do I," she whispered, a hint of longing in her voice.

He reached into his pocket and pulled out a small piece of paper, sliding it across the table toward her. "My address," he said softly. "Come by tonight, if you want. No pressure, but... I'd like to see you. Away from here, where we don't have to be so careful."

Mae picked up the paper, her fingers brushing his as she did. "I'll think about it," she replied, trying to sound casual, but her heart was already racing at the thought.

"Do," he urged, his eyes holding hers. "And if you come, I promise you won't regret it."

She nodded, tucking the paper into her pocket. "I'll see," she said, though she already knew she would go.

He smiled one last time, a look that made her heart flutter, and then he was gone, leaving her alone with her thoughts, the sound of the cafe murmuring around her. She stayed there for a few minutes, trying to steady her breath, trying to decide if she was brave enough to follow through.

Later that evening, Mae stood outside his building, her hands shoved deep into her pockets, her breath visible in the cool night air. She looked up at the windows, the light glowing softly from inside. Her heart pounded in her chest, a mixture of nerves and anticipation. She knew this was a line she was about to cross, a decision that would change everything. But she was drawn to him, pulled by a force she couldn't resist.

She took a deep breath and climbed the stairs, her footsteps echoing in the narrow hallway. She found his door, her hand hovering for a moment before she knocked softly. A moment later, the door opened, and there he was, his expression lighting up when he saw her.

"Mae," he breathed, stepping aside to let her in. "I wasn't sure if you'd come."

"Neither was I," she replied honestly, stepping inside, the warmth of the room wrapping around her like a blanket.

He closed the door behind her, turning the lock with a soft click that seemed to echo in the quiet space. "I'm glad you did," he murmured, his voice low and husky.

She looked around, taking in the room — the bookshelves overflowing with volumes, the soft lighting, the faint smell of sandalwood. It felt intimate, private, like a world apart from everything else. "It's nice," she said softly, turning back to face him.

He smiled, stepping closer, his eyes darkening with a familiar hunger. "You're nice," he replied, his hand reaching out to touch her cheek, his thumb grazing her skin with a tenderness that made her heart skip a beat.

She felt her breath catch, her body leaning into his touch. "I've been thinking about you," she whispered, her voice barely audible.

"And I've been thinking about you," he replied, his hand sliding down to cup her chin, lifting her face to his. "Every moment since you walked into my class."

He leaned down, his lips capturing hers in a slow, deliberate kiss, his hands moving to her waist, pulling her closer. She melted into him, her arms wrapping around his neck, her body pressing against his. His kiss was a promise, a taste of something deeper, and she felt herself giving in, letting go of all the doubts, all the fears.

His hands moved up her back, sliding under her shirt, his touch warm and firm. She felt a tremor run through her, a soft moan escaping her lips. "Michael," she whispered against his mouth, her fingers tangling in his hair.

He groaned softly, his lips moving to her neck, kissing a line down to her collarbone. "I want you," he murmured, his breath hot against her skin. "Here, now. No more hiding."

Her body responded instantly, a surge of heat coursing through her veins. "Yes," she whispered, her voice filled with longing.

He pulled her closer, his hands sliding to her hips, lifting her effortlessly. She wrapped her legs around his waist, feeling the solid strength of him beneath her. He carried her to the couch, lowering her down gently, his body pressing against hers, his mouth never leaving her skin.

He kissed her deeply, his hands exploring, touching, learning every curve, every soft place. She felt herself unraveling under his touch, her body arching toward him, her breath coming in ragged gasps. "I need you," she whispered, her voice a soft plea.

His hands moved to her jeans, unbuttoning them with deft fingers, sliding them down her legs. "And I need you," he replied, his voice rough with desire. "More than I've ever needed anyone."

He moved over her, his body pressing hers into the cushions, his mouth finding hers in a kiss that was both fierce and tender.

She felt herself let go, felt the world outside fade away until there was nothing but him — his touch, his taste, his breath mingling with hers. It was more than she had imagined, more intense, more consuming.

They moved together, their bodies finding a rhythm, a dance of skin against skin, breath against breath. She felt herself slipping over the edge, her body tensing, her breath catching in her throat as she reached for him, holding on as if he were the only solid thing in a world spinning out of control. His hands gripped her tighter, fingers pressing into her hips, guiding her, urging her on.

Her back arched, a soft cry escaping her lips, and he silenced it with a deep kiss, swallowing the sound, his mouth hungry against hers. She felt a wave build inside her, powerful and unstoppable, cresting higher with each touch, each thrust. His breath was hot against her neck, his voice a low, raspy whisper in her ear, urging her on, telling her how beautiful she was, how much he wanted her.

"Let go," he murmured, his lips brushing her ear, his voice like velvet. "Let go for me, Mae."

His words were a trigger, unlocking something deep within her, and she felt herself surrender, felt the tension release in a rush of heat and light. Her body convulsed, her nails digging into his shoulders, a moan breaking free from her throat as she came apart in his arms. He held her through it, his movements steady, his body never letting her go, keeping her grounded as the waves of pleasure crashed over her.

And then he was right there with her, his own release following hers, a deep groan rumbling in his chest as he buried his face in her neck, his body shuddering against hers. She felt his warmth spread through her, felt him tremble, and she held *him close, her arms wrapping around him, pulling him in as if she could fuse their bodies together, as if she could hold onto this moment forever.*

For a long time, they lay there, tangled in each other, their breathing heavy, their bodies slick with sweat. Mae felt a sense of peace settle over her, a quiet calm that she hadn't realized she was missing. She felt his heartbeat against her chest, strong and steady, and she realized that, despite the risks, despite the danger, this felt right. He felt right.

Michael's hand stroked her hair, his touch gentle now, his breathing slowing. "Mae," he whispered, his lips brushing against her forehead, "I've wanted this for so long."

She looked up at him, her fingers tracing the line of his jaw, her eyes searching his. "Me too," she confessed softly, her voice still breathless. "I didn't think... I didn't think it would feel like this."

He smiled, a soft, almost boyish grin that made her heart flutter. "Like what?" he asked, his thumb brushing over her bottom lip, his touch light, tender.

"Like..." She paused, searching for the right words. "Like I've found something I didn't even know I was looking for."

He kissed her again, slower this time, his lips lingering on hers, savoring the moment. "You have," he murmured against her mouth. "We both have."

They lay there for a few more moments, the weight of what they had just done sinking in. She knew they couldn't stay like this forever, that the world outside this room would intrude soon enough, with all its rules and judgments. But for now, in this quiet, intimate space, she felt safe, she felt wanted, she felt... alive.

Michael finally pulled back, his eyes dark and intense as he looked at her. "I don't want this to end," he said quietly, his voice filled with something that sounded almost like fear. "But we have to be careful, Mae. No one can know about us."

She nodded, understanding the gravity of his words. "I know," she whispered. "I promise, I won't tell anyone."

He smiled, a small, sad smile that tugged at her heart. "Good," he said softly, his fingers brushing her cheek. "We'll find a way to make this work. I don't know how yet, but I can't... I can't let you go."

Mae felt a surge of emotion at his words, a mix of hope and fear, desire and doubt. "I don't want you to," she replied, her voice firm, her resolve clear. "I want this. I want you."

His smile widened, his hand cupping her face, his thumb brushing over her cheekbone. "Then we'll make it work," he promised, his voice filled with a quiet determination. "No matter what."

She nodded, a small smile breaking across her lips. "No matter what," she echoed.

They stayed like that for a few more minutes, their bodies pressed close, their breaths mingling, before reality began to creep back in. Michael sighed, his fingers threading through her hair one last time before he pulled away, reaching for a blanket to cover them both. "We should get some rest," he murmured, a hint of reluctance in his voice. "It's late."

Mae nodded, snuggling closer to him, feeling the warmth of his body seep into hers. "Just a little longer," she whispered, closing her eyes, letting herself drift in the comfort of his arms.

And as they lay there, in the quiet of his small apartment, Mae knew that whatever happened next, whatever challenges they faced, she wouldn't regret this. Not for a moment. She had taken a leap, crossed a line, and she wasn't looking back.

Chapter 4: Whispers in the Halls

The morning light filtered through the thin curtains of Michael's apartment, casting soft shadows on the walls. Mae stirred, slowly waking from a sleep that had been deep and dreamless. She felt Michael's arm draped over her, his body warm against hers. For a moment, she lay still, savoring the quiet intimacy of the moment, the feeling of safety in his embrace.

But the world outside had already started to intrude. A distant car honked; a bird sang on the windowsill. She knew she had to leave soon, return to her dorm before her absence was noticed, before questions were asked that she couldn't answer. She sighed softly, her fingers tracing the line of his jaw, feeling the roughness of his morning stubble.

Michael stirred, his eyes fluttering open. He smiled sleepily at her, his hand moving to cup her cheek. "Morning," he murmured, his voice rough with sleep.

"Morning," she whispered back, leaning in to kiss him softly. The kiss was gentle, lingering, a reminder of the night they had shared. But as their lips parted, reality came rushing back. She pulled away slightly, a frown tugging at the corners of her mouth.

"I should go," she said reluctantly, glancing at the clock on his bedside table. "I have an early class."

Michael nodded, his expression shifting to something more serious. "I understand," he replied, sitting up and running a hand through his tousled hair. "But I want to see you again... soon."

Mae smiled, feeling her heart lift at his words. "I want that too," she admitted. "But we need to be careful. If anyone finds out..."

He nodded, a shadow passing over his face. "I know. We'll keep things quiet. Discreet." He reached out, his fingers brushing hers. "But we'll make it work, Mae. We have to."

She nodded, squeezing his hand before reluctantly pulling away. She dressed quickly, trying not to think too much about what lay ahead, the risks they were taking. She paused at the door, looking back at him, taking in the sight of him — rumpled, sleepy, but undeniably hers, at least for now.

"I'll see you soon," she whispered, and he nodded, his eyes soft, watching her until the door closed behind her.

Back on campus, Mae moved quickly through the halls, keeping her head down, hoping not to draw attention. But as she rounded the corner near her dorm, she heard a voice — low, hushed, but unmistakably talking about her.

"...saw her leaving his office the other day," a girl whispered to her friend, her voice barely more than a murmur, but Mae's ears caught every word. "And again, yesterday. They seemed... close."

Mae's heart skipped a beat, her steps faltering. She pressed herself against the wall, trying to stay out of sight, her pulse quickening. She had been so careful, hadn't she? But still, somehow, people were talking.

"Who?" the other girl asked, sounding intrigued. "Mae? The one from the farm?"

"Yeah, her," the first girl confirmed. "With Professor Arden. I mean, maybe it's nothing, but... they looked a little too friendly, you know?"

Mae felt a cold sweat break out on her skin. Her stomach twisted with anxiety. How had they noticed? She'd thought they were being so careful, so discreet. She waited, holding her breath until the girls moved on, their voices fading as they walked away.

She slipped out from her hiding spot, her mind racing. The rumors were starting, and it wouldn't take much for them to spiral out of control. She needed to be even more cautious, needed to make sure no one could confirm what was going on. Her heart pounded in her chest as she made her way to her next class, her mind spinning with possibilities, with fears.

But as the day wore on, the whispers seemed to follow her. She caught snippets of conversation — people mentioning her name, looking at her with curiosity, with something close to suspicion. She felt exposed, like everyone could see right through her, could see what she had done, what she was doing.

By the time her last class ended, she was tense, her nerves frayed. She needed to talk to Michael, needed to figure out what to do. She waited until the hall was clear, then made her way to his office, her steps quick, purposeful.

When she reached the door, she knocked softly, her breath catching in her throat. After a moment, Michael opened it, his expression brightening when he saw her. But his smile faded quickly when he saw the worry in her eyes.

"Mae, what's wrong?" he asked, his voice low, concerned.

"People are talking," she whispered, stepping inside and closing the door behind her. "They've noticed us. They're saying things... about you and me."

Michael's face tightened, a frown creasing his brow. "Damn," he muttered under his breath. "I thought we were being careful."

"We were," she insisted, her voice tense. "But I heard them today, in the hall. They're suspicious, Michael. I don't know how, but they are."

He sighed, running a hand through his hair, his expression conflicted. "Okay," he said finally, his voice steady. "We need to calm down. This doesn't mean they know anything for sure. It's just rumors, whispers. We can handle this."

Mae nodded, but she felt a tremor of fear run through her. "But what if they do find out? What if they tell someone? A professor? The dean?"

Michael moved closer, his hands resting on her shoulders, his touch firm but gentle. "Listen to me," he said softly, his eyes searching hers. "We'll be careful. More careful. No more meetings on campus, no more... public displays."

She nodded again, swallowing hard, trying to steady her breath. "Okay," she agreed, though her heart was still pounding. "But... what if that's not enough?"

He hesitated, his expression softening. "Then we'll deal with it," he replied, his voice low. "But Mae, I don't want to lose this. I don't want to lose you."

She felt her heart swell at his words, but the fear was still there, lurking just beneath the surface. "I don't want to lose you either," she whispered, leaning into his touch.

He pulled her into his arms, holding her close, his hand stroking her hair. "We'll find a way," he murmured. "I promise you, Mae, we'll find a way."

She nodded, resting her head against his chest, feeling the steady beat of his heart. "Okay," she whispered, her voice barely audible. "I trust you."

They stayed like that for a long moment, wrapped in each other, trying to draw strength from their connection. But Mae knew that things were changing, that their world was becoming more precarious. The whispers had started, and it was only a matter of time before the truth — or something close to it — came out.

And as much as she wanted to hold onto this, to him, she knew they were standing on the edge of a precipice. One wrong move, one slip, and everything could come crashing down.

Chapter 5: The Walls Close In

The rumors spread like wildfire. What had started as hushed whispers in the hallways quickly grew louder, more insistent, twisting into something uglier, more damaging. Mae felt it everywhere she went — the sidelong glances, the knowing smirks, the half-hidden grins. She felt eyes on her in every room, felt the weight of judgment pressing down, growing heavier with each passing day.

She tried to focus on her classes, tried to keep her head down and ignore the murmurs, but it was like trying to ignore a storm raging around her. Her friends began to ask questions, their expressions curious, concerned. "Mae, is everything okay?" one of them asked during lunch, her eyes wide with worry. "I heard some things... about you and Professor Arden."

Mae's heart clenched, her stomach twisting into knots. "It's nothing," she lied, forcing a smile, though her hands were trembling under the table. "Just stupid rumors, you know how people talk."

Her friend didn't look convinced but nodded slowly. "Okay," she said softly, "but if you need to talk... I'm here."

Mae nodded, grateful but terrified, her mind spinning with the implications. She excused herself soon after, unable to bear the weight of her friend's worried gaze any longer. She needed to talk to Michael, needed to figure out what to do. The whispers were getting louder, and she could feel the walls closing in around her.

That evening, she found herself outside Michael's building once again, her heart racing as she knocked on his door. He opened *it quickly, his face tense, his eyes shadowed. "Mae," he breathed, pulling her inside. "I was worried you wouldn't come."*

"I had to," she replied, her voice tight. "Michael, it's getting worse. People are talking. They're asking questions."

He nodded, closing the door behind her, his expression grim. "I know," he said quietly. "I've heard things too. Some of the faculty... they've noticed."

Mae's stomach dropped, fear coursing through her. "What do you mean?" she asked, her voice trembling.

Michael sighed, running a hand through his hair. "Nothing concrete," he reassured her, "but they've seen us talking, lingering after class. They're starting to ask why. They're wondering if there's something... inappropriate going on."

"And what did you say?" she pressed, her heart pounding in her chest.

"I brushed it off," he replied, his voice firm. "I told them you were struggling with the material, that I was just helping you out. But they're watching us now, Mae. We have to be even more careful."

Mae nodded, anxiety clawing at her insides. "What do we do?" she whispered, her voice small, desperate.

He took her hands in his, squeezing them gently. "We keep our distance, for a while," he suggested reluctantly. "No more meeting on campus. No more... public displays."

Mae felt a pang of disappointment, but she knew he was right. "Okay," she agreed softly, though the thought of being apart from him, of pretending there was nothing between them, made her heart ache.

Michael pulled her closer, his arms wrapping around her, holding her tight. "It's just temporary," he murmured into her hair. "Just until things calm down. I don't want to lose you, Mae. Not because of some stupid rumors."

She nodded against his chest, her eyes stinging with unshed tears. "I don't want to lose you either," she whispered, her voice barely audible.

They stood like that for a long moment, wrapped in each other's arms, trying to draw strength from their connection. But Mae knew this wasn't over. The rumors were only getting louder, and the scrutiny was only going to get worse.

The next day, Mae walked into her literature class with a sense of dread pooling in her stomach. She kept her eyes down, trying to avoid the curious stares, the whispers that seemed to follow her everywhere. She took her usual seat in the back, her hands gripping the edge of her desk so tightly her knuckles turned white.

Michael entered the room a few minutes later, his expression neutral, his eyes sweeping across the students before landing on her for the briefest moment. His face gave nothing away, but Mae could feel the tension radiating from him, could sense the tightness in his shoulders, the strain in his posture.

He began the lecture, his voice steady, calm, as if nothing was amiss. But Mae noticed the way his eyes flickered toward her more often than usual, the way his fingers tapped against his notebook, betraying his nerves.

And then, halfway through the class, the door swung open, and a tall woman with sharp eyes and a no-nonsense expression stepped in. The room fell silent as everyone turned to look at her. Michael paused mid-sentence, his brow furrowing as he looked at the intruder.

"Dean Caldwell," he greeted, his voice calm but tense. "Can I help you with something?"

The woman nodded, her gaze sweeping over the students before settling on Michael. "I need a word with you, Professor Arden," she said, her tone clipped, businesslike.

Michael's jaw tightened, but he nodded. "Of course," he replied, setting his notes down on the desk. "Class, continue with your reading," he instructed, before following the dean out of the room, the door closing behind them with a soft click.

Mae's heart pounded in her chest, a wave of panic rising in her throat. She stared at the door, unable to concentrate on the words in front of her, her mind racing with possibilities. What did the dean want? Did she know?

Minutes ticked by, each one feeling like an eternity. Mae could barely breathe, her hands trembling as she fumbled with her pen, trying to keep her focus, trying to ignore the dread that was spreading through her.

Finally, after what felt like hours, Michael returned. His expression was tight, his eyes dark with frustration. He resumed the lecture without a word, but Mae could see the tension in his jaw, the way his hands clenched into fists at his sides.

When the class ended, Mae lingered, waiting until everyone else had left. She approached Michael cautiously, her heart in her throat. "What happened?" she asked quietly, her voice barely more than a whisper.

He glanced around, making sure they were alone, before sighing heavily. "The dean is... concerned," he said carefully. "She's heard the rumors, and she's worried about the university's reputation. She warned me to be cautious, to avoid any... impropriety."

Mae's stomach dropped, her worst fears confirmed. "What does that mean?" she asked, her voice trembling.

Michael's expression softened, his eyes filled with concern. "It means we need to be more careful than ever," he replied. "It means... no more private meetings, at least not for a while. It means we have to act like nothing is happening, like we're just teacher and student."

Mae felt a wave of despair wash over her. "I don't know if I can do that," she whispered, tears welling in her eyes.

Michael reached out, his hand brushing her arm, his touch sending a spark through her. "I know it's hard," he said softly, "but we have to. For now, at least. We have to protect ourselves, Mae. I promise you, it won't be like this forever. Just... give it time."

She nodded, though her heart felt heavy, her chest tight. "Okay," she whispered, though the word felt hollow. "I'll try."

He gave her a small, sad smile. "That's all we can do," he murmured. "Just try."

Mae left the classroom, her mind spinning, her heart aching. She felt like she was walking a tightrope, balancing on a thin line between desire and disaster. She knew she wanted him, needed him, but the risks were becoming too great. The walls were closing in, and she wasn't sure how much longer she could keep up the facade.

And as she walked away, the whispers seemed to follow her, louder than ever, echoing in her ears like a warning she couldn't ignore.

Chapter 6: The Strain of Silence

The days felt longer now, stretching into an eternity. Mae moved through them like a shadow, her steps quiet, her presence subdued. The whispers hadn't stopped; if anything, they'd grown louder. She heard them everywhere — in the hallways, the dining hall, even during lectures. They were like a low, constant hum, always present, always there, buzzing in her ears, clawing at her nerves.

She avoided eye contact, kept to herself, hoping that if she stayed small, unnoticed, the rumors would fade. But she felt the weight of curious stares pressing on her back, the judging eyes of classmates and strangers alike. Her friends grew more distant, their concern turning to suspicion, their smiles fading into wary glances. She felt a sense of isolation creeping in, curling around her like a fog.

Michael had become a ghost in her life. He was there, in her thoughts, in her dreams, but in reality, he kept his distance. In class, he spoke to her like any other student, his tone neutral, his gaze carefully avoiding hers. When they passed each other on campus, he gave a small nod, a polite smile, but nothing more. The barrier between them felt like a wall of glass — transparent but unbreakable.

Mae felt the strain of it, the silence between them growing louder with each passing day. She missed him desperately — his touch, his voice, the way he made her feel seen, understood. She craved the moments they had stolen, the intimacy they had shared. But now, all she had were memories and a deep, aching emptiness that seemed to grow inside her like a wound.

One afternoon, as she sat in the library, trying to focus on her studies, she felt her phone vibrate in her pocket. Her heart leapt as she pulled it out, hoping it might be him. Her fingers trembled as she unlocked the screen, and her breath caught when she saw his name.

Michael: *Meet me tonight. Usual place. Midnight.*

Mae's heart raced, a surge of relief and fear coursing through her veins. She glanced around, half-expecting someone to see the message, to know her secret. But no one was looking at her. She quickly typed back a reply.

Mae: *I'll be there.*

The hours crawled by after that, each one slower than the last. She felt the anticipation building inside her, a tight coil of nerves and longing. When midnight finally approached, she slipped out of her dorm, moving quietly, her steps light on the worn carpet. She kept her head down, her eyes scanning the shadows, making sure no one saw her.

When she reached the small, hidden alcove near the old science building — their "usual place" — she saw him waiting, his back against the wall, his hands tucked into his pockets. The moonlight cast a soft glow over his face, highlighting the lines of worry etched into his features. But when he saw her, his expression softened, a small smile playing at the corners of his mouth.

"Mae," he murmured, his voice low and warm. "I wasn't sure you'd come."

"I couldn't stay away," she whispered, moving closer. "I've missed you."

He reached for her, pulling her into his arms, his hands sliding around her waist, his face burying in her hair. "I've missed you too," he confessed, his breath warm against her ear. "More than I can say."

She felt a rush of emotion, her eyes stinging with unshed tears. "This is so hard," she whispered, her voice breaking. "I hate pretending, hiding... it feels like we're losing ourselves."

Michael sighed, his hands tightening around her, his lips pressing against her forehead. "I know," he murmured. "I hate it too. But we have to be careful. For now, at least. Until things calm down."

"What if they never do?" she asked, pulling back to look up at him. "What if this never gets easier?"

He looked at her, his expression pained. "Then we have to make a choice," he said softly. "But I'm not ready to let go, Mae. Not yet. I don't think I ever will be."

Mae nodded, her heart aching. "I don't want to let go either," she whispered. "I'm trying to be strong, but it's hard. So hard."

He cupped her face in his hands, his thumbs brushing away the tears that had started to fall. "You are strong," he said firmly. "Stronger than you know. We'll find a way through this, Mae. We have to."

She nodded again, her hands gripping his shirt, pulling him closer. "I just... I don't know how much longer I can keep pretending," she confessed, her voice small, vulnerable.

He kissed her, a soft, slow kiss that tasted of longing and need, of promises unspoken. "You don't have to pretend with me," he whispered against her lips. "Not ever."

She melted into his embrace, feeling the tension drain from her body, if only for a moment. His hands roamed her back, pulling her closer, his mouth moving to her neck, kissing a line down to her collarbone. She sighed, a sound of relief and desire, her hands tangling in his hair.

But the fear was still there, lurking at the edges of her mind, a shadow that wouldn't fade. "Michael," she murmured, her voice shaking, "I'm scared."

He pulled back slightly, his eyes searching hers. "I know," he said softly. "I'm scared too. But I won't let anything happen to you. I promise."

She nodded, trying to believe him, trying to hold onto his words like a lifeline. "Okay," she whispered. "Okay."

They stood there for a long moment, holding each other, letting the silence wrap around them like a cocoon. The world outside felt distant, unreal. Here, in his arms, she felt safe, felt like maybe they could find a way through the darkness. But she knew they couldn't stay like this forever.

"We should go," he finally said, his voice reluctant. "Before someone sees us."

Mae nodded, pulling away slowly, her fingers lingering on his arm. "When will I see you again?" she asked, her voice filled with a quiet desperation.

He hesitated, then sighed. "Soon," he promised. "I'll find a way."

She nodded, though her heart sank. "Okay," she whispered, stepping back. "I'll wait."

He watched her for a moment, his eyes dark and intense, as if memorizing every detail of her face. "Be careful," he murmured. "Please."

"I will," she replied, her voice steady, even as her heart ached. "You too."

He nodded, giving her one last, lingering look before turning and disappearing into the shadows. Mae watched him go, her chest tight, her breath shallow. She felt like she was balancing on the edge of a knife, every step precarious, every move a risk.

And as she turned to head back to her dorm, she felt a sense of dread settle over her, a feeling that something was coming, something she couldn't see, something she couldn't stop.

The next morning, as Mae sat in the dining hall, picking at her breakfast, she felt a tap on her shoulder. She turned to see one of her classmates, a girl she barely knew, standing there, her expression curious, her eyes sharp.

"Hey, Mae," the girl said, her voice casual but probing. "Can I ask you something?"

Mae felt her heart rate quicken, a sense of unease creeping in. "Sure," she replied, forcing a smile. "What is it?"

The girl leaned in slightly, her voice dropping to a whisper. "Is it true... about you and Professor Arden?"

Mae felt her stomach twist, her hands tightening around her coffee cup. "What do you mean?" she asked carefully, trying to keep her voice steady.

"I heard some things," the girl continued, her eyes narrowing. "People are saying you're... close. Like, really close."

Mae's mind raced, her pulse pounding in her ears. She took a deep breath, trying to steady herself. "People like to talk," she said lightly, shrugging. "But there's nothing going on. Just rumors."

The girl nodded slowly, but her expression remained skeptical. "If you say so," she said, her tone laced with doubt. "But you should be careful, Mae. People are watching."

Mae forced another smile, her heart hammering in her chest. "Thanks for the advice," she replied, her voice tight. "But there's nothing to worry about."

The girl gave a small shrug, then walked away, leaving Mae alone with her thoughts. She felt a cold sweat break out on her skin, her stomach churning. She needed to find Michael, needed to tell him that people were getting closer to the truth, that they were running out of time.

Chapter 7: Shadows in the Light

Mae couldn't shake the feeling of dread that clung to her like a second skin. Everywhere she went, it was there — a low hum of anxiety, a sense of impending doom that shadowed her every step. The whispers hadn't stopped; if anything, they'd grown sharper, more pointed. She could feel them slicing through the air around her, threatening to unravel everything.

Her heart felt heavy, weighed down by the constant fear of discovery, the relentless pressure of keeping up appearances. She'd been avoiding Michael as much as possible, as they'd agreed, but every moment apart felt like a slow torture, a reminder of what they were risking and what they stood to lose.

She found herself moving mechanically through her days, attending classes, completing assignments, but all of it felt distant, like she was watching her own life from behind a thick pane of glass. Her mind was always elsewhere — on him, on their stolen moments, on the way his touch had felt against her skin, on the way he'd whispered her name.

And now, she was waiting. Waiting for another message, another midnight meeting. Waiting for any sign that they could return to each other, even if just for a little while.

It came late one evening, just as she was about to give up hope. Her phone buzzed in her pocket, and she snatched it up, her heart leaping into her throat. The message was short, simple:

Michael: *Tonight. Same place. Midnight.*

Mae's fingers flew across the screen, her reply instant.

Mae: *I'll be there.*

As midnight approached, Mae made her way toward the old science building, her steps light, her breath quick. The campus was mostly deserted, the shadows long and deep in the moonlight. She felt her pulse quicken with every step, a mix of excitement and fear thrumming through her veins.

When she arrived at their usual spot, she found Michael already there, leaning against the wall, his face partially hidden in the shadows. He looked up as she approached, a small smile breaking across his face.

"You came," he murmured, relief evident in his voice.

"Of course I did," she replied softly, moving closer. "I've missed you."

He reached for her, his hands sliding around her waist, pulling her close. "I've missed you too," he whispered, his breath warm against her ear. "So much."

For a moment, they simply held each other, their bodies pressed together in the darkness, their hearts beating in time. But the weight of their situation was still there, pressing down on them, an invisible barrier they couldn't ignore.

"Things are getting worse," Mae whispered, her voice tight with worry. "People are talking more. Asking questions."

Michael nodded, his expression grim. "I know," he replied. "I've heard things too. There's talk among the faculty... and I think someone might be watching us."

Mae's heart skipped a beat. "Watching us?" she echoed, her voice a mix of fear and disbelief. "Who?"

"I don't know," he admitted, his brow furrowing. "But I've noticed things — people lingering outside my office, strange looks during meetings. It's like they're waiting for us to slip up."

Mae felt a shiver run down her spine, the weight of their predicament pressing in on her from all sides. "What do we do?" she asked, her voice barely above a whisper.

Michael sighed, his hands tightening on her waist. "I don't know," he said softly. "But we need to be more careful than ever. No more late-night meetings like this. It's too risky."

Mae felt a pang of disappointment, but she knew he was right. "Okay," she agreed reluctantly. "But I don't want to stop seeing you. I can't."

He pressed his forehead against hers, his breath warm on her skin. "I don't want to stop either," he murmured. "But we need to be smart. We need to find a way to be together without drawing attention."

She nodded, feeling a knot of fear tighten in her chest. "I'll do whatever it takes," she whispered. "I don't want to lose you."

Michael kissed her, a soft, lingering kiss that sent a shiver down her spine. "You won't," he promised against her lips. "We'll find a way. I swear it."

They held each other for a few more moments, savoring the closeness, the quiet. But the world outside felt too close, too threatening. They both knew this couldn't last.

"I should go," Michael said finally, his voice filled with regret. "Before someone sees us."

Mae nodded, her heart heavy. "Okay," she whispered. "But... soon?"

He smiled, though it didn't reach his eyes. "Soon," he agreed. "I'll find a way."

She watched him disappear into the shadows, her heart aching, her mind spinning with a thousand possibilities, each one darker than the last.

The next morning, Mae felt the tension mounting even before she reached her first class. She sensed it in the way people stared at her, in the way conversations seemed to quiet when she passed by. There was a charge in the air, something heavy and electric, and she felt it prickling against her skin.

As she walked toward her lecture hall, she noticed a small group of students clustered together, their heads bent in close conversation. They glanced up as she approached, their eyes narrowing, and she felt a wave of anxiety wash over her.

"That's her," she heard one of them whisper, just loud enough for her to catch.

Mae's steps faltered, her stomach twisting. She kept her eyes forward, trying to ignore the stares, the murmurs, but she could feel the weight of their attention pressing down on her like a physical force.

She reached the lecture hall and slipped inside, her hands shaking as she took her seat. She tried to calm her racing heart, tried to focus on anything but the whispers, but it was impossible. The room felt too small, too crowded, and she could feel the walls closing in.

When Michael entered, his expression was unreadable, his gaze sweeping over the room, lingering on her for just a moment before moving on. He began his lecture, his voice steady, but Mae could see the tension in his shoulders, the tightness in his jaw.

Halfway through, the door opened, and Dean Caldwell stepped in. Mae's heart plummeted into her stomach, a wave of cold fear washing over her. She watched as the dean crossed the room, her expression stern, her eyes focused on Michael.

"Professor Arden," Dean Caldwell said, her tone clipped. "May I have a word with you outside?"

Michael nodded, his face carefully neutral. "Of course, Dean Caldwell," he replied, setting his notes aside. "Class, continue with the reading."

Mae watched him follow the dean out of the room, her heart pounding in her chest. She could feel a cold sweat break out on her skin, a knot of dread tightening in her stomach. She couldn't breathe, couldn't think. What did the dean want? What was she going to say?

The minutes ticked by, each one feeling like an eternity. Mae tried to focus on the text in front of her, but the words blurred together, meaningless shapes on the page. All she could think about was Michael, about the dean, about what might be happening just outside the door.

When Michael finally returned, his face was pale, his expression strained. He resumed the lecture, but his voice was tight, his eyes hard. Mae could see the worry etched into his features, the fear lurking just beneath the surface.

When the class ended, she lingered, waiting until everyone else had left. She approached him slowly, her heart in her throat. "What happened?" she asked quietly, her voice barely more than a whisper.

He glanced around, making sure they were alone, before speaking. "The dean wants me to take a leave of absence," he said, his voice low and controlled. "She says there have been too many complaints, too many... concerns about my conduct."

Mae's stomach twisted, a wave of nausea washing over her. "What does that mean?" she asked, her voice shaking.

Michael sighed, running a hand through his hair. "It means I have to step back," he replied. "At least for a while. Until this all blows over. If it ever does."

Mae felt her world tilt, her breath catching in her throat. "But... what about us?" she whispered, her eyes filling with tears.

He reached for her, his hand brushing her arm, his touch gentle but firm. "We'll figure it out," he murmured. "I'm not giving up on us, Mae. But we have to be careful. More careful than ever."

She nodded, tears slipping down her cheeks. "I'm scared, Michael," she confessed, her voice breaking.

He pulled her into his arms, holding her tight. "I know," he whispered. "But we'll get through this. I promise."

They stayed like that for a long moment, wrapped in each other's arms, trying to draw strength from their connection. But Mae knew that things were changing, that their world was becoming more precarious with every passing day.

Chapter 8: Under the Microscope

The days blurred together, each one heavier than the last. Mae felt like she was moving through a fog, every step slow, every breath labored. The whispers hadn't stopped — they'd only grown louder, sharper, cutting deeper. The walls were closing in, and the pressure was becoming unbearable.

Michael's leave of absence had become the newest topic of conversation, the rumors swirling like smoke in the air, thick and suffocating. Mae heard bits and pieces everywhere she went: speculation about his sudden disappearance, questions about his conduct, theories that ranged from the absurd to the disturbingly close to the truth.

"He's probably involved in something," someone whispered in the library. "I heard it's with a student."

"Did you hear about Arden?" a girl murmured to her friend in the dining hall. "They say he's being investigated for misconduct."

Mae felt each word like a blow, a sharp sting that left her breathless, her stomach churning. She wanted to scream, to shout at them that they didn't know anything, that they were wrong. But she couldn't. She had to keep her head down, had to stay quiet, had to pretend she was just another student, unaffected, unaware.

But inside, she was breaking. She hadn't heard from Michael since he'd been asked to leave. No messages, no calls, nothing. The silence was deafening, a void that swallowed her whole. She wanted to reach out, wanted to find him, but she knew it was too dangerous. She couldn't risk drawing more attention to herself, to them.

And so, she waited. Waited for a sign, a signal, anything to tell her that he was okay, that they were okay. But as the days stretched on, her hope began to fade, replaced by a gnawing sense of dread.

One afternoon, as Mae sat in the library, trying to focus on an assignment, she saw a shadow fall across her table. She looked up to see Dean Caldwell standing there, her expression unreadable, her eyes cold and assessing.

"Mae," the dean said, her voice clipped and formal. "May I have a word with you in my office?"

Mae felt her heart stop, her blood turning to ice in her veins. She nodded slowly, her hands trembling as she gathered her things. "Of course, Dean Caldwell," she replied, trying to keep her voice steady, calm.

She followed the dean through the library, down the hall, and into her office. The room was small, cluttered with books and papers, but Mae barely noticed. All she could feel was the pounding of her heart, the fear tightening in her chest.

The dean closed the door behind them and motioned for Mae to sit. "Please," she said, her tone polite but firm. "Have a seat."

Mae sat down, her hands folded tightly in her lap, her fingers digging into her palms. She waited, her breath shallow, her eyes fixed on the dean.

Dean Caldwell took her seat behind the desk, her expression serious, her gaze fixed on Mae. "I'm sure you're aware of the rumors circulating around campus," she began, her voice measured. "About Professor Arden."

Mae nodded, her mouth dry. "Yes," she whispered, her voice barely audible. "I've heard them."

The dean's eyes narrowed slightly. "And are you also aware that there have been... concerns raised about his relationship with a student?" she continued, her tone pointed.

Mae felt a wave of panic rise in her chest, her stomach twisting painfully. "I... I've heard things," she admitted, choosing her words carefully. "But I don't know anything for sure."

Dean Caldwell leaned forward slightly, her gaze sharp, penetrating. "Mae," she said softly, "I want you to be honest with me. If there is anything going on, anything inappropriate, it's important that we address it now."

Mae's heart raced, her mind spinning with possibilities, with fears. She wanted to deny it, to lie, but she knew the dean was watching her closely, weighing every word, every gesture.

"There's nothing inappropriate," she said finally, her voice steadier than she felt. "Professor Arden was just... helping me with my studies. That's all."

The dean's expression didn't change. "Helping you with your studies," she repeated slowly, her tone skeptical. "And yet, several people have noted that you two seemed... closer than that."

Mae swallowed hard, her hands gripping the edge of her chair. "I don't know what they saw," she replied, her voice tight. "But it wasn't anything more than that. I swear."

For a moment, the dean said nothing, her eyes boring into Mae's. Then she nodded slowly, leaning back in her chair. "Very well," she said quietly. "But Mae, I need you to understand something. The university takes these matters very seriously. If there is any truth to these rumors, any evidence of misconduct, there will be consequences. For both of you."

Mae nodded, her throat tight, her hands trembling. "I understand," she whispered.

Dean Caldwell's expression softened slightly. "I hope you do," she said. "Because I don't want to see a promising student like you get caught up in something that could jeopardize your future."

Mae forced a small smile, though her stomach was in knots. "I appreciate that," she replied, her voice strained.

The dean nodded once more. "You're free to go," she said, her tone dismissive. "But Mae, if there's anything you need to tell me, anything at all, my door is always open."

Mae nodded quickly, standing up on shaky legs. "Thank you, Dean Caldwell," she murmured, before turning and making her way out of the office as quickly as she could.

The moment she was outside, she felt the tears sting her eyes. She hurried to a quiet corner of the campus, her breath coming in short, panicked gasps. Her mind was racing, her heart pounding. She felt trapped, cornered, like an animal with no way out.

What should she do? Should she tell Michael? Could she even reach him? She needed to warn him, to let him know that the dean was digging, that they were running out of time. But she had no way of contacting him, no idea where he was, no clue what to do next.

She felt a wave of helplessness crash over her, a crushing sense of despair. She leaned against the cold stone wall, her fingers digging into the rough surface, her breath hitching in her throat. She had never felt so alone, so afraid.

But then, as if in answer to her silent plea, her phone buzzed in her pocket. She pulled it out, her heart leaping into her throat when she saw his name on the screen.

Michael: *We need to meet. Urgent. Same place, tonight. Midnight.*

Mae's fingers trembled as she typed out a reply.

Mae: *I'll be there.*

That night, as Mae made her way toward their usual meeting spot, her mind raced with questions, with fears. She kept to the shadows, moving quickly, her breath coming in short, shallow bursts. She had to see him, had to warn him. She had to find out what he knew.

When she reached the alcove, Michael was already there, his face tense, his eyes shadowed. He looked up as she approached, his expression softening with relief. "Mae," he breathed, pulling her into his arms. "Thank God."

"Michael," she whispered, holding onto him tightly, "the dean... she spoke to me today. She's asking questions, probing."

He nodded, his jaw tight. "I know," he replied. "I've heard from a colleague. They're looking for something — anything to prove their suspicions."

"What do we do?" Mae asked, her voice filled with fear. "They're closing in on us."

Michael sighed, his hands cupping her face, his thumbs brushing her cheeks. "We have to be smart," he said softly. "We can't give them any reason to suspect us. No more meetings, no more messages. We have to lie low, just for a little while."

"But what if they find out anyway?" she asked, her eyes wide with panic.

He pulled her closer, his lips brushing against her forehead. "Then we deal with it," he murmured. "But for now, we have to be careful. Mae, I'm not going to let them ruin us. I promise."

She nodded, tears slipping down her cheeks. "I'm scared," she whispered. "I'm so scared."

He held her tighter, his arms wrapping around her, his voice steady and calm. "I know," he whispered. "But we'll get through this. Together."

They stood like that for a long time, holding each other, trying to find solace in their connection. But Mae knew that things were getting worse, that they were running out of time. The shadows were closing in, and the noose was tightening.

And as they stood there in the darkness, she couldn't shake the feeling that they were standing on the edge of a precipice, teetering dangerously close to the fall.

Chapter 9: Beneath the Surface

Mae felt like she was living on borrowed time. Every minute seemed to stretch into hours, every glance held the weight of suspicion, and every conversation felt like a trap waiting to spring. The days were heavy with tension, a suffocating cloak that wrapped tighter with each breath she took. She could hardly sleep, her nights filled with restless tossing, dreams blurring into nightmares where everything she loved was ripped away.

She tried to focus on her studies, but the words on the pages seemed to shift and blur. Her mind was elsewhere — on Michael, on the dean, on the whispered conversations she could never quite make out. She felt the world closing in around her, each step she took feeling like one closer to the edge of a cliff.

Michael had kept his distance as promised, but the absence was agony. She missed him fiercely — his touch, his voice, the way he could make her feel safe even when the world was falling apart. And though she knew they needed to be careful, the silence was unbearable.

One afternoon, as she walked to the dining hall, she spotted a group of students gathered near the notice board, their heads bent in close conversation. She felt her heart skip a beat, a familiar dread creeping in. She slowed her steps, trying to catch a fragment of their discussion.

"...suspended indefinitely," one of them said, their voice tinged with excitement. "It's all over campus."

Mae's stomach twisted. She edged closer, trying to listen without drawing attention to herself.

"I heard they found something," another whispered. "Emails, maybe. Or messages. Something that proves it."

Mae felt a wave of panic rise in her chest. Emails? Messages? Her mind raced back to the texts she and Michael had exchanged, the messages that now felt like a noose tightening around their necks. Had someone seen them? Had they been caught?

She felt her pulse quicken, her breath coming faster. She needed to find out more, needed to know exactly what was happening. She turned and hurried toward the administration building, her steps quick, purposeful.

The receptionist gave her a curious glance as she approached the desk, but Mae tried to keep her expression neutral, calm. "Excuse me," she said, her voice steady, "I need to speak with Dean Caldwell."

The receptionist raised an eyebrow. "Do you have an appointment?" she asked, her tone polite but firm.

"No, but it's urgent," Mae replied, hoping her urgency would sway the woman. "Please, I just need a few minutes."

The receptionist hesitated, then sighed. "Wait here," she said, standing up and disappearing into the back office.

Mae waited, her heart pounding, her palms damp with sweat. She glanced around, feeling like every eye in the room was on her, like every whisper was about her. She felt exposed, vulnerable, like a spotlight had been turned on her secrets.

A moment later, the receptionist returned, her expression neutral. "The dean will see you now," she said, gesturing toward the open door.

Mae nodded, swallowing hard as she made her way into the office. Dean Caldwell was seated behind her desk, her expression unreadable, her hands folded neatly in front of her.

"Mae," the dean greeted, her tone calm but firm. "What can I do for you?"

Mae took a deep breath, trying to steady herself. "I've been hearing... things," she began carefully. "About Professor Arden. About his suspension. I wanted to know if they're true."

The dean's eyes narrowed slightly, her gaze sharpening. "I see," she said slowly. "And why, exactly, are you concerned about Professor Arden's suspension?"

Mae hesitated for a moment, choosing her words carefully. "I just... I wanted to make sure he was okay," she replied, trying to sound casual, concerned. "He's been a great teacher, and I know how rumors can be."

Dean Caldwell's expression remained unchanged. "Mae," she said slowly, "I hope you understand that this is a serious matter. Professor Arden's conduct is under investigation, and until it is resolved, I cannot discuss the details with you or anyone else."

Mae's heart sank, but she nodded. "I understand," she murmured, her voice small. "But... is there anything I can do? Anything I can say?"

The dean's gaze sharpened further. "Why would there be anything you could say, Mae?" she asked, her tone probing. "Is there something you know that you haven't told us?"

Mae felt a cold sweat break out on her skin, her stomach twisting with fear. "No," she said quickly, too quickly. "I just... I wanted to help."

The dean leaned back in her chair, her eyes never leaving Mae's. "If you have nothing to say, Mae, then I suggest you focus on your studies and leave this matter to the administration," she replied, her tone dismissive. "We'll handle it from here."

Mae nodded, her hands shaking slightly. "Of course," she whispered. "Thank you, Dean Caldwell."

She turned and left the office, her heart pounding in her chest, her mind spinning with questions. She felt more confused than ever, more lost. She didn't know what to do, who to trust, or how to protect the man she loved from whatever was coming.

That night, Mae sat in her dorm room, staring at her phone, willing it to ring, to buzz, to do anything. She needed to hear from Michael, needed to know he was okay. But there was nothing — just silence, thick and oppressive.

She thought about sending a message, but every time her fingers hovered over the keys, she hesitated. What if someone was watching? What if they were tracing their conversations? She couldn't risk it, couldn't take that chance. Not when everything felt so precarious.

Just as she was about to give up, there was a soft knock at her door. Mae's heart leapt into her throat, her pulse racing. She stood up, crossing the room quickly, and opened the door a crack.

Standing there, in the dim hallway, was a girl she recognized from one of her classes — Jess, a quiet student who always sat in the back, kept to herself. But tonight, her eyes were wide, her face pale.

"Mae," Jess whispered urgently, glancing over her shoulder. "Can I come in?"

Mae hesitated, her mind racing. "What is it?" she asked, her voice cautious.

"Please," Jess insisted, her voice low and hurried. "I need to talk to you. It's important."

Mae nodded and opened the door wider, letting Jess slip inside. She closed it quickly behind her, turning to face her with a mixture of curiosity and dread. "What's going on?" Mae asked, her voice tight.

Jess took a deep breath, her hands trembling. "I heard something today," she said, her voice low. "Something about you... and Professor Arden."

Mae felt her heart stop, her blood turning to ice. "What did you hear?" she asked, her voice barely more than a whisper.

Jess glanced around the room, as if making sure they were alone. "There's a student," she whispered. "A guy named Tom. He's been telling people that he saw you and Professor Arden... together. Late at night, near the old science building."

Mae's stomach dropped, a wave of nausea washing over her. "What?" she breathed, her mind spinning. "How does he know?"

Jess shook her head, her eyes wide. "I don't know," she replied. "But he's talking. A lot. And people are listening."

Mae felt a cold sweat break out on her skin. "Why are you telling me this?" she asked, her voice shaking.

Jess hesitated, then sighed. "Because... I think they're going to use it against you," she whispered. "I heard some of the faculty talking. They're looking for a reason to expel you, Mae. To make an example."

Mae's breath caught in her throat, fear clawing at her insides. "Oh God," she whispered, her voice breaking. "What do I do?"

Jess reached out, her hand gripping Mae's arm. "You need to be careful," she urged. "Stay away from him. Don't give them any more reason to come after you. And whatever you do, don't talk to Tom. Don't give him any more ammunition."

Mae nodded, her heart racing. "Thank you," she whispered, her voice thick with emotion. "Thank you for telling me."

Jess nodded, her expression serious. "Just... be careful," she repeated. "I don't want to see you get hurt."

Mae nodded again, her eyes stinging with tears. "I will," she promised. "I'll be careful."

Jess gave her a small, worried smile before slipping back out into the hallway, leaving Mae alone with her thoughts, her fears. She felt a wave of despair wash over her, a sinking feeling in her chest. She was trapped, cornered, and she didn't know how to get out.

She needed to warn Michael, needed to tell him what was happening. But how? She couldn't send a message, couldn't call. Not now. Not when they were both under a microscope, every move scrutinized.

Her mind raced, her heart pounding. She felt the panic rising, her breath coming faster, her chest tightening. She had to think, had to find a way. But every path seemed blocked, every option filled with risk.

And as she sat there, alone in the darkness, she couldn't shake the feeling that time was running out, that the walls were closing in faster than ever, and that they were about to be caught in a trap from which there was no escape.

Chapter 10: Dangerous Moves

Mae's hands trembled as she paced the floor of her dorm room, her mind spinning with a thousand thoughts. She needed to get in touch with Michael, needed to warn him about Tom, but every option felt like a trap. She couldn't text or call — the risk was too high. If someone was already watching their communications, any direct contact could be the final nail in their coffin.

She paused, running her hands through her hair, trying to think. She needed a plan, something that wouldn't raise suspicion. Something discreet. And then, slowly, an idea began to form.

She grabbed her backpack and a pen, quickly scribbling a note on a scrap of paper:

"Meet me at the old greenhouse. 11 PM. We need to talk. — M"

She folded it carefully, slipped it into her pocket, and headed out the door. Her heart raced as she walked across campus, every glance over her shoulder filled with paranoia. She made her way to the administrative building, where the faculty mailboxes were kept. The building was mostly deserted this time of day, just a few stray students and staff moving through.

She slipped inside and moved quickly, trying to look casual, just another student running an errand. When she reached the row of faculty mailboxes, she scanned the names until she found Michael's. Taking a deep breath, she slipped the note through the narrow slot, her fingers lingering for a moment before she pulled them back.

She turned and left the building, her heart pounding in her chest. Now, all she could do was wait.

Hours passed like days. Mae couldn't focus, couldn't think. She tried to keep herself busy, but her mind kept drifting back to the note, to the risk she'd taken. She kept glancing at the clock, willing the time to move faster.

Finally, as the clock neared 11 PM, she made her way toward the old greenhouse on the far side of campus. The building was ancient, long abandoned, its glass panes fogged and cracked, the once-lush plants inside now withered and dry. It was the perfect place — hidden, forgotten, far from prying eyes.

She pushed open the creaky door, stepping into the darkness. The air was cold, filled with the scent of damp earth and decay. She took a deep breath, trying to steady her nerves, listening for any sound, any sign of movement.

And then she heard it — the soft crunch of footsteps on broken glass. She turned, her heart racing, and saw Michael stepping through the shadows, his expression tense, his eyes scanning the room.

"Mae," he whispered, moving toward her. "I got your note. What's going on?"

She rushed into his arms, relief flooding through her. "Michael, it's worse than we thought," she murmured, her voice shaking. "There's a student — Tom. He's been telling people that he saw us together. He knows, Michael. And the dean... she's digging for something, anything."

Michael's jaw tightened, his hands gripping her shoulders. "Damn it," he muttered under his breath. "I knew there was talk, but this... it's happening faster than I expected."

"What do we do?" Mae asked, her eyes wide with fear. "They're closing in on us, Michael. I don't know how much longer we can keep this up."

He took a deep breath, his eyes narrowing in thought. "We have to be strategic," he said slowly. "If they're looking for proof, we need to make sure they don't find any. No more messages, no more meetings on campus. We lay low, make it seem like there's nothing to find."

Mae nodded, but her fear didn't lessen. "What about Tom?" she whispered. "If he keeps talking..."

Michael's expression darkened. "Leave him to me," he said quietly. "I'll find a way to handle it."

Mae's heart fluttered with worry. "Michael, be careful," she urged. "I don't want you getting into more trouble."

He smiled, but it didn't reach his eyes. "I will," he promised. "But I'm not going to let this kid ruin everything. Not when we've come this far."

They stood there in the dim light, holding each other, their breaths mingling in the cold air. Mae felt a small measure of comfort in his arms, but the fear was still there, lurking at the edges of her mind.

"We should go," Michael said finally, pulling back. "Before someone sees us."

Mae nodded, reluctant to let him go. "Okay," she whispered. "But... when will I see you again?"

He hesitated, his eyes softening. "Soon," he murmured. "I'll find a way. Just... be careful, Mae. Please."

"You too," she replied, her voice barely audible.

He kissed her softly, a lingering kiss that made her heart ache, before slipping back into the shadows. Mae watched him go, her stomach twisting with a mix of fear and hope. She turned and left the greenhouse, her steps quick and light, her breath coming in short, nervous bursts.

The next day, Mae kept her head down, moving quietly through the halls, trying to avoid any attention. She couldn't stop thinking about Michael, about Tom, about the dean. Every glance felt like a challenge, every whispered conversation seemed to be about her.

She made her way to the library, hoping to find some quiet, some space to think. But as she turned a corner, she nearly collided with someone — Tom.

He looked at her, his eyes narrowing, a sly smile playing at his lips. "Mae," he greeted, his voice smooth, casual. "How are you?"

Mae felt her pulse quicken, her muscles tensing. "I'm fine," she replied shortly, trying to keep her voice steady. "Just... busy."

"Busy with what?" he asked, his tone light, but his eyes sharp. "Or should I say... with whom?"

Mae felt a flush creep up her neck. "What do you mean?" she asked, her voice tight.

Tom leaned in slightly, his smile widening. "I think you know exactly what I mean," he murmured. "I've seen you, Mae. I've seen you with him."

Mae swallowed hard, her heart racing. "You don't know anything," she said, her voice sharper than she intended.

Tom chuckled softly, a dangerous glint in his eyes. "Maybe not," he conceded, "but others will believe what I say. And I'm sure the administration would be very interested to hear what I have to say."

Mae felt a wave of panic wash over her. "Why are you doing this?" she demanded, her voice rising. "What do you want?"

Tom's smile faded, his expression turning cold. "I want the truth," he replied. "And if you don't give it to me, I'll find another way to get it."

Mae felt a surge of fear, but she forced herself to stay calm. "There is no truth to find," she insisted. "It's just rumors."

Tom shrugged, unconvinced. "We'll see," he said lightly. "But you should know, Mae... I'm not going to stop until I get what I want."

He turned and walked away, leaving Mae standing there, her heart pounding, her hands shaking. She felt trapped, cornered, like an animal caught in a snare.

She needed to talk to Michael, needed to tell him what had happened. But how? They'd agreed to stay out of contact, to avoid any suspicion. She felt panic rising in her chest, her breath coming in short, shallow gasps.

But then, an idea formed in her mind, desperate but necessary. She'd find a way to speak to him without drawing attention, without leaving a trace. She had to warn him, had to let him know that Tom was getting closer, that the danger was real.

She took a deep breath, steadying herself. She'd find a way. She had to.

That evening, Mae waited until the campus was quiet, until the shadows had lengthened and the lights had dimmed. She made her way to the old science building, slipping inside through a side door, her heart racing.

She found the small, dark room where Michael had once taught late-night seminars, a place she knew well. She took a piece of chalk from the board and wrote a simple message on the wall:

"**Meet me tomorrow night. 10 PM. Near the library steps. Urgent.**"

She stepped back, her heart pounding, hoping he'd see it, hoping he'd understand. She erased the message quickly, then left the room, her steps quiet and measured. She moved through the shadows, her mind racing, her heart filled with a mix of fear and determination.

She had to warn him. She had to protect them both. She just hoped it wasn't too late.

Chapter 11: The Unraveling

Mae's nerves were frayed, every fiber of her being on high alert. She spent the day on edge, her mind replaying the conversation with Tom over and over. She kept glancing at her phone, checking the time, counting down the hours until 10 PM. The uncertainty was eating at her, gnawing away like a persistent itch she couldn't scratch.

She felt a growing sense of urgency. Her message to Michael had been a risk — a big one — but she had no other choice. If Tom was intent on exposing them, she needed to act fast. She needed to know what Michael was thinking, how they could maneuver around this latest threat.

As the day crawled by, Mae tried to keep herself busy, moving from class to class, sitting in the back of the library with a book she couldn't read. Her eyes scanned the pages, but her mind was elsewhere, tangled in a web of fear and desperate hope.

When the clock finally neared 10 PM, Mae slipped out of the library and made her way toward the meeting spot near the library steps. The night air was cool, a slight breeze rustling the leaves. She felt her heart pounding in her chest, her hands clammy with sweat.

She moved into the shadows, leaning against the stone wall, her eyes scanning the darkness for any sign of movement. Every rustle, every distant voice made her jump, her nerves stretched thin.

And then, she saw him. Michael emerged from the far side of the library, his steps quick, his face partially obscured by the dim light. When he reached her, he pulled her into the shadows, his hands gripping her shoulders tightly.

"Mae," he whispered urgently, his eyes searching hers. "What's going on? What did you find out?"

"Tom," she replied, her voice hushed, "he's been telling people he saw us together. He's threatening to go to the administration. He wants to expose us, Michael."

Michael's expression darkened, his jaw clenching. "I figured as much," he muttered. "He's been hanging around, asking questions, trying to stir things up."

"What do we do?" Mae asked, panic creeping into her voice. "We can't keep dodging this forever."

Michael took a deep breath, his hands moving to cup her face, his thumbs brushing her cheeks. "We need to turn the tables," he said quietly. "If Tom wants to make this a game, we play it better. We give him something else to focus on."

Mae frowned, confusion clouding her features. "What do you mean?"

"A distraction," Michael explained. "Something that makes his story less credible, less believable. We make him look like he's just trying to cause trouble, not expose the truth."

"But how?" Mae asked, uncertainty clear in her voice.

"Leave that to me," Michael replied, his tone firm. "I've been thinking... there's a way to discredit him, to make him look like a liar. But it's risky."

Mae's heart skipped a beat. "Risky how?"

Michael hesitated, his eyes darkening. "It involves getting close to him," he said slowly. "Finding out what he really wants, why he's doing this. We need leverage, something that makes him back down."

"Close to him?" Mae repeated, her stomach tightening. "You mean... talk to him?"

Michael nodded. "Yes, but carefully," he replied. "I've heard things about Tom, things that could work in our favor if we handle it right. But you have to be careful, Mae. Don't give him any reason to suspect you're onto him."

Mae felt a wave of fear, but she nodded. "Okay," she whispered. "I'll do it. But what if he doesn't back down?"

Michael's grip tightened on her shoulders. "Then we escalate," he said softly. "We make sure the administration knows he's not to be trusted. We create enough doubt to muddy the waters."

Mae swallowed hard, the weight of his words settling heavily on her. "Okay," she agreed. "I'll find a way to talk to him, to get close."

Michael leaned in, pressing a soft kiss to her forehead. "Be careful," he whispered. "I don't want you getting hurt. If anything feels off, you get out, understand?"

Mae nodded, her heart pounding. "I will," she promised. "But we have to do something, Michael. We can't let him ruin us."

He pulled her into a tight embrace, his lips brushing her ear. "We won't," he murmured. "We're in this together."

They stood there for a moment longer, holding each other in the darkness, before Michael pulled back. "I have to go," he said quietly. "I'll be in touch soon. Just... be careful."

Mae nodded, watching as he slipped back into the shadows. She felt a mix of fear and determination welling up inside her. She knew what she had to do, but the path ahead felt treacherous, filled with unseen dangers.

The next day, Mae set her plan into motion. She knew she had to find a way to get close to Tom without arousing suspicion. She waited until after her morning class, then approached him in the hallway, her expression carefully neutral.

"Hey, Tom," she greeted, trying to sound casual. "Got a minute?"

Tom looked up, surprised, his eyes narrowing slightly. "Mae," he replied slowly, a smirk playing at his lips. "What can I do for you?"

Mae forced a smile, her stomach churning. "I just... I wanted to clear the air," she said. "I've heard some things, and I thought it would be better if we talked directly."

Tom's smirk widened. "Heard some things?" he repeated, amusement in his voice. "Like what?"

Mae swallowed hard, maintaining her composure. "Like... you've been telling people you saw me with Professor Arden," she said carefully. "I just wanted to know why."

Tom chuckled, leaning against the wall. "Why? Because I did see you," he replied. "And because I don't like secrets, Mae. I think people have a right to know what's going on."

"And what do you think is going on?" Mae asked, keeping her tone light, curious.

"Oh, I have my theories," Tom replied, his eyes glinting with something Mae didn't like. "But maybe you can tell me the truth. You and Arden... you're more than just teacher and student, aren't you?"

Mae felt her heart race, but she forced herself to remain calm. "We're not what you think," she said softly. "But I get it — you're curious. Maybe you're just looking for a little... excitement?"

Tom raised an eyebrow, intrigued. "What are you getting at, Mae?" he asked, his tone playful.

Mae took a deep breath, stepping a little closer. "I just think... maybe we could help each other," she suggested. "If you want to know more, we can talk. But not like this. Not in the open."

Tom studied her, his expression thoughtful. "Interesting," he murmured. "Okay, Mae. I'm listening. Where and when?"

"Tonight," she replied quickly, her mind racing. "At the coffee shop near the east gate. 8 PM. We can talk then."

Tom nodded slowly, a satisfied grin spreading across his face. "Alright," he agreed. "I'll be there. Let's see what you have to say."

Mae forced another smile, her nerves jangling. "Great," she said, turning to leave. "See you tonight."

As she walked away, she felt a rush of adrenaline, fear coursing through her veins. She had no idea if her plan would work, if she could really get close to Tom without exposing herself. But she had to try. For Michael. For them.

That evening, Mae arrived at the coffee shop early, her heart hammering in her chest. She found a quiet table in the corner, her eyes darting to the door every few seconds. She had rehearsed her lines, planned her approach, but now that she was here, the fear was creeping in, making her doubt.

When Tom finally walked in, his gaze immediately found hers. He sauntered over, a cocky grin on his face, and slid into the chair across from her. "Alright, Mae," he drawled, "let's hear it. What's this all about?"

Mae took a deep breath, steadying herself. "I think we've gotten off on the wrong foot," she began carefully. "I know you're looking for something... and I want to help you find it."

Tom leaned back, amused. "Help me find what?" he asked.

"The truth," Mae said, her voice firm. "But it's not what you think it is."

Tom's eyes gleamed with interest. "Go on," he urged.

Mae leaned in slightly, her voice dropping to a whisper. "I'll tell you everything," she promised. "But only if you agree to back off. Stop spreading rumors. Stop talking to the administration."

Tom smirked, clearly enjoying the game. "And why would I do that?"

Mae's expression didn't waver. "Because if you don't, I'll make sure everyone knows what I know about you," she replied smoothly. "And trust me, it won't be pretty."

Tom's smile faltered for a moment, but he quickly recovered. "You're bluffing," he accused, but there was a hint of doubt in his voice.

"Try me," Mae shot back, holding his gaze steady.

For a long moment, they stared at each other, the tension thick between them. Finally, Tom leaned forward, his expression serious. "Fine," he said quietly. "You've got my attention. What do you know?"

Mae smiled, her heart racing, but she kept her voice steady. "Let's just say I know enough," she replied. "Now, are you going to listen, or are we done here?"

Tom leaned back, a thoughtful look on his face. "Alright," he conceded, "I'm listening. But this better be good."

Mae nodded, a small spark of hope flickering in her chest. "Oh, it will be," she promised. "I'll make sure of it."

As they continued their tense negotiation, Mae felt a strange calm settle over her. She didn't know if this would work, if she could really turn the tables on Tom. But for the first time in days, she felt like she had a little bit of control, a little bit of power.

And she intended to use it, no matter what it took.

Chapter 13: Forbidden Fire

Mae woke up the next morning feeling a strange mixture of anxiety and exhilaration. Her email had been sent, and now all she could do was wait. The tension of not knowing what would happen next was like a live wire under her skin, sparking with every passing moment. She felt exposed, vulnerable, but also oddly empowered. She had made her move, and now the game was in motion.

She went about her day, trying to keep a low profile, but her mind kept wandering back to Michael. It had been days since they last spoke, days filled with whispers and threats, and she was desperate to see him, to feel his touch, to remind herself why they were fighting so hard to stay together. She felt the distance between them like a physical ache, a need that gnawed at her, deep and relentless.

By midday, the campus was buzzing. Mae could feel the change in the air, the tension crackling around her. She overheard snippets of conversations — students talking about the email, about the rumors of the administration's investigation. It seemed like her message had reached the right people, and the campus was alive with speculation.

But she also heard other things, things that made her stomach twist with fear. Whispers about Tom meeting with the dean, about faculty members being asked to provide statements, about a special committee that had been convened to "get to the bottom of things." Mae knew she had stirred the pot, but now she was worried she might have pushed too far, too fast.

She needed to see Michael, needed to feel his arms around her, to hear his voice tell her it would be okay. And she needed it now.

That evening, Mae made her way to the secluded corner of campus where they had often met in secret, behind the old science building. She paced nervously in the shadows, her breath coming in short, anxious bursts. She had sent a quick note to Michael earlier, a simple message in chalk on the back of a bench near his building: "Meet me at 9. Usual place."

She waited, her heart pounding, and then she saw him. Michael approached from the shadows, his expression tense, his steps quick and purposeful. As soon as he reached her, he pulled her into his arms, his hands gripping her tightly, as if he was afraid she might disappear.

"Mae," he murmured, his voice rough with emotion. "God, I've missed you."

Mae melted into his embrace, feeling a rush of relief, of longing. "I've missed you too," she whispered, her hands running up his back, pulling him closer. "So much."

He pressed his forehead against hers, his breath hot on her skin. "I'm sorry I've been so distant," he whispered. "I was trying to protect you, to keep us safe."

"I know," she replied softly, "but I can't do this without you. I need you, Michael. I need to feel you."

His eyes darkened with desire, and he leaned in, capturing her lips in a deep, hungry kiss. Mae felt her body ignite, the tension of the past days melting away under the heat of his touch. His hands slid down her back, pulling her closer, his fingers digging into her waist as if he could fuse their bodies together.

She moaned softly against his mouth, her hands moving to tangle in his hair, her body pressing against his with a desperate need. "Michael," she breathed, "I don't care about the risks anymore. I just want you."

He groaned, his lips moving to her neck, kissing a trail down to her collarbone, his hands roaming her body with a rough, insistent urgency. "I want you too," he murmured against her skin, his breath hot and ragged. "God, I've been going crazy without you."

Mae felt a surge of desire, her body aching for him, for his touch. "Then take me," she whispered, her voice trembling with need. "Take me right here."

Michael pulled back slightly, his eyes searching hers, filled with a mix of hunger and concern. "Are you sure?" he asked, his voice low and husky. "Right here, right now?"

She nodded, her heart beating fast. "Yes," she whispered, her hands sliding under his shirt, feeling the hard muscles of his back. "I need you, Michael. I need you now."

He didn't need any more encouragement. He kissed her again, harder this time, his hands moving to her hips, lifting her slightly as he pressed her against the cold stone wall of the building. Mae gasped, feeling the roughness of the stone against her back, the heat of his body against hers.

His hands slid up her thighs, pushing her skirt higher, his fingers tracing the edge of her panties. She moaned, her body arching toward him, her breath coming in short, desperate gasps. "Michael," she whispered, her voice a mix of plea and demand. "Please."

He groaned softly, his fingers slipping under the fabric, teasing her, making her shiver with anticipation. "You're so beautiful," he murmured, his lips moving back to her neck, kissing her skin, his breath hot and ragged. "So perfect."

Mae felt herself spiraling, her body responding to his every touch, every kiss. She wrapped her legs around his waist, pulling him closer, deeper, her hands gripping his shoulders, holding on as if her life depended on it.

He moved against her, his body firm and insistent, his hands sliding under her blouse, caressing her skin, his touch sending shivers down her spine. "Tell me you want this," he whispered, his voice rough with desire.

"I want this," she breathed, her voice trembling with need. "I want you."

He kissed her deeply, his hands moving with purpose, his body pressing hers into the wall, his mouth claiming hers in a kiss that left her breathless. She felt herself letting go, giving in to the sensations coursing through her, her body arching against his, needing more, wanting everything.

His hands found the hem of her skirt, pulling it up, his fingers sliding under her panties, finding her wet and ready. "God, Mae," he groaned, his lips brushing her ear, his breath hot against her skin. "You drive me crazy."

"Then show me," she whispered, her voice a mix of challenge and need. "Show me how much."

He smiled against her lips, a wicked, satisfied smile. "Oh, I will," he promised, his hands moving with purpose, his lips capturing hers in a kiss that left her breathless, wanting, aching for more.

He took her there, against the wall, his body moving with hers in a rhythm that felt like a dance, a surrender to the fire that had been burning between them for so long. Mae felt herself spiraling, her body trembling, her breath catching in her throat as she reached for him, holding on as if he were the only solid thing in a world spinning out of control.

And in that moment, nothing else mattered — not the whispers, not the threats, not the world that seemed determined to tear them apart. All that mattered was him, his touch, his breath, the way he made her feel alive in a way she had never felt before.

When it was over, they stood there for a long moment, their bodies pressed together, their breaths mingling in the cool night air. Michael held her close, his hands gentle now, his lips brushing her forehead. "Mae," he murmured softly, "I don't want to lose you."

She looked up at him, her fingers tracing the line of his jaw, her heart swelling with emotion. "You won't," she whispered, her voice filled with quiet determination. "I promise."

He kissed her again, slower this time, his lips lingering on hers, savoring the moment. "We'll get through this," he murmured against her mouth. "Together."

Mae nodded, her heart racing, her body still tingling from their intimacy. "Together," she echoed softly.

They knew the risks, knew the dangers, but in that moment, it didn't matter. All that mattered was each other, the fire that burned between them, the love that made them willing to fight for what they had, no matter what it took.

And as they stood there, wrapped in each other's arms, they knew that whatever came next, they would face it together, united in their desire, their defiance, their love.

Chapter 14: The Edge of Revelation

*M*ae lay awake in her dorm room, the events of the previous night replaying in her mind like a vivid, sensuous dream. Her body still hummed with the memory of Michael's touch, the heat of his kisses, the way he had made her feel alive, like nothing else in the world mattered. She felt a strange, exhilarating mix of fear and excitement coursing through her veins, her skin still tingling from where his hands had been.

But as dawn began to break, the cold light of reality crept back in, and the anxiety returned, gnawing at her insides. The whispers on campus had not gone quiet — if anything, they seemed louder. She felt eyes on her everywhere she went, felt the tension in the air growing thicker, the threat of exposure looming ever closer.

She needed to know what was happening with the administration, what Jess had found out. She needed to stay one step ahead, to keep her and Michael safe. And she needed to see him again, to feel his arms around her, to reassure herself that they were still together in this, still willing to fight.

Mae decided to take action. She found Jess in the dining hall later that morning, sitting alone with a book, her expression tense and focused. Mae slid into the seat across from her, her voice low and urgent.

"Jess," she said, leaning forward, "do you have any news? Did you hear anything more about the meeting?"

Jess looked up, her face serious, her voice a whisper. "Yes," she replied. "I spoke to my contact in the administration. The meeting is happening today, this afternoon. They're planning to discuss the investigation, to see if there's enough evidence to move forward."

Mae's heart pounded in her chest. "And do they have anything?" she asked, her voice trembling. "Anything solid?"

Jess hesitated, then shook her head. "No, not yet," she answered. "But they're looking for something, anything. They think there's more to this than meets the eye."

"We have to stop them," Mae whispered fiercely. "We have to find a way to make them back off."

Jess nodded, her expression grim. "I've been thinking," she said slowly. "Maybe we can create a distraction, something to make them look somewhere else, to doubt their own suspicions."

"Like what?" Mae asked, desperate for a solution.

"We could... spread a rumor," Jess suggested cautiously. "Something big, something that shifts the focus away from you and Michael. Something that makes them question everything."

Mae considered this, her mind racing. "But what kind of rumor?" she asked. "It has to be believable."

Jess leaned in, lowering her voice. "Maybe we suggest that someone in the administration has a grudge against Michael," she proposed. "Make it seem like the investigation is biased, that there's a personal vendetta at play."

Mae nodded slowly, a spark of hope igniting in her chest. "That could work," she murmured. "If we make it look like they're targeting him unfairly, it could create enough doubt."

"Exactly," Jess agreed. "We just need to make sure it spreads quickly, gets into the right ears."

Mae felt a surge of determination. "I'll start talking," she said. "I know a few people who like to gossip. We can plant the seed and see if it grows."

Jess smiled, a glimmer of excitement in her eyes. "Okay," she replied. "But be careful. If they find out we're behind it, it could make things worse."

"I will," Mae promised. "Thank you, Jess. I don't know what I'd do without you."

Jess shrugged, a faint smile tugging at her lips. "Just... be careful, Mae," she said. "We're playing a dangerous game."

Mae nodded, feeling a mix of fear and resolve. She knew the risks, knew they were dancing on the edge of disaster. But she had to do something, had to keep fighting. For Michael. For herself. For them.

That afternoon, Mae moved through campus with a new purpose, her eyes scanning for the right people, the ones who could help her spread the rumor. She started with a few casual conversations, dropping hints, making small comments about how the administration seemed overly interested in Michael, how it seemed personal.

She could see the curiosity spark in their eyes, the way they leaned in a little closer, wanting to hear more. She kept her tone light, her words carefully chosen, planting the seeds of doubt without making it too obvious.

By the end of the day, she could feel the shift in the air. The whispers were changing, the conversations shifting focus. She heard snippets of speculation — "I heard they're out to get him," "Someone in the administration has it out for him," "It's all a setup."

She felt a flicker of hope, a sense of control returning. Maybe, just maybe, they could turn this around.

As the sun began to set, she knew she had to see Michael again, to tell him what she'd done, to feel his touch once more. She sent him a quick message using their new discreet method — a small note slipped into his faculty mailbox: "Meet me at the old greenhouse. 10 PM."

That night, Mae waited in the old greenhouse, her heart pounding with anticipation. The air was cool and damp, filled with the scent of earth and decay. She felt a shiver of nerves, her skin prickling with a mix of fear and excitement.

And then she saw him. Michael slipped in through the broken door, his expression tense, his eyes scanning the darkness until they found her. He crossed the space quickly, pulling her into his arms, his hands gripping her tightly.

"Mae," he breathed, his voice rough with emotion. "What's going on? What have you done?"

Mae leaned into his touch, feeling the warmth of his body against hers, the comfort of his arms. "I spread a rumor," she confessed softly. "About the administration, about them targeting you. I think it's working. I think people are starting to doubt."

Michael's eyes widened, a mix of surprise and concern. "Mae, that's risky," he whispered. "If they find out, they could come down even harder on us."

"I know," she replied, her voice firm. "But we had to do something. We couldn't just sit back and wait for them to destroy us."

He sighed, his hands moving to cup her face, his thumbs brushing her cheeks. "I know," he murmured, "but I'm worried about you. I don't want you getting hurt."

"I don't care," Mae whispered, her voice filled with fierce determination. "I just want to be with you, Michael. I want to feel you."

Michael's eyes darkened with desire, and he leaned in, capturing her lips in a deep, passionate kiss. Mae felt the fire ignite between them, the tension of the past days melting away under the heat of his touch. His hands slid down her back, pulling her closer, his fingers pressing into her skin.

She moaned softly against his mouth, her body arching toward him, her hands tangling in his hair. "Michael," she breathed, "I need you."

He groaned, his lips moving to her neck, kissing a trail down to her collarbone, his hands roaming her body with a rough, insistent urgency. "I need you too," he murmured against her skin, his breath hot and ragged. "God, I can't get enough of you."

Mae felt a surge of desire, her body aching for him, for his touch. "Then take me," she whispered, her voice trembling with need. "Take me right here."

He didn't hesitate. He kissed her harder, his hands moving to lift her onto an old, dusty table, his body pressing against hers. Mae gasped, feeling the cool wood against her back, the heat of his body between her legs.

His hands slid up her thighs, pushing her skirt higher, his fingers tracing the edge of her panties. She moaned, her body arching toward him, her breath coming in short, desperate gasps. "Michael," she whispered, her voice a mix of plea and demand. "Please."

He pulled her panties down slowly, his eyes locked on hers, his expression hungry, intense. "You're so beautiful," he murmured, his hands exploring her skin, his touch firm and sure. "So perfect."

Mae felt herself spiraling, her body responding to his every touch, every kiss. She wrapped her legs around his waist, pulling *him closer, her hands gripping his shoulders, holding on as if her life depended on it.*

He moved against her, his body firm and insistent, his hands sliding under her blouse, caressing her skin, his touch sending shivers down her spine. "Tell me you want this," he whispered, his voice rough with desire.

"I want this," she breathed, her voice trembling with need. "I want you."

He kissed her deeply, his hands moving with purpose, his body pressing hers into the table, his mouth claiming hers in a kiss that left her breathless. She felt herself letting go, giving in to the sensations coursing through her, her body arching against his, needing more, wanting everything.

His hands found her hips, guiding her against him, their movements growing faster, more urgent. Mae could feel the strength of his desire in every touch, every breath, as his fingers gripped her tighter, pulling her closer with a raw, unrestrained need. She gasped, her hands clutching his shoulders, her body instinctively moving with his, meeting each thrust with a hungry rhythm of her own. The intensity between them built like a wave, cresting higher and higher, threatening to spill over. The pressure, the heat, the desperate connection between them felt almost unbearable.

"Michael," she whispered, her voice breaking with emotion, "don't stop... please."

He growled softly in response, his lips brushing against her ear, his breath hot and uneven. "I won't," he promised, his voice a low, raspy murmur that sent shivers down her spine. "I can't... I need you, Mae... all of you."

His mouth found hers again in a searing kiss, their tongues entwining, and she felt herself surrender completely to him, her body trembling as he drove deeper, filling her completely. Her nails dug into his back, and she clung to him like he was the only thing keeping her grounded, her soft moans mixing with his ragged breathing. The tension coiled tighter in her core, her pulse quickening, her heart pounding like a drumbeat in her ears. She could feel him everywhere — his hands, his mouth, his breath, his body — and it felt like nothing else in the world existed but this moment, this connection, this wild, reckless passion.

The world around them seemed to blur, time losing all meaning. Mae felt herself reaching the edge, her body tightening, her breath coming in short, desperate gasps. Michael's hands gripped her hips harder, his movements more forceful, his eyes locked onto hers with a blazing intensity.

"Come for me, Mae," he murmured against her lips, his voice raw with need. "Let go... let me feel you."

And with those words, she shattered, her body convulsing as a wave of pleasure crashed over her, her cry of release muffled by his mouth as he kissed her through it. Her world exploded into light and color, every nerve ending alive, tingling, her body trembling with the force of her climax.

Michael held her tight, his own body tensing, his grip on her firm as he found his release with a deep, guttural groan, his forehead resting against hers, their breaths mingling in the cool air of the greenhouse. They stayed like that for a long moment, bodies entwined, hearts racing, the heat of their passion slowly ebbing away.

He whispered her name like a prayer, his lips brushing her temple, his hands cradling her face. "Mae... oh, Mae," he breathed, his voice filled with a mixture of wonder and longing. "You're everything to me."

Mae opened her eyes, meeting his gaze, her own filled with emotion. "I feel the same," she whispered, her fingers tracing the line of his jaw. "I don't know what's going to happen, but I know I want you... always."

He smiled softly, kissing her again, slower this time, as if savoring every moment. "We'll find a way," he promised, his voice tender yet determined. "No matter what... we'll find a way."

She nodded, feeling a warmth spread through her chest, a flicker of hope amidst the uncertainty. "Together," she murmured, leaning into his touch, letting herself believe, if only for a moment, that they could indeed find a way to make this work.

And as they stood there, wrapped in each other's arms, the world outside felt distant, the danger forgotten. In that moment, it was just them, just their love, their bodies still entwined, their hearts beating as one. The fire between them burned bright, defiant, and unquenchable, a light in the darkness.

Chapter 15: The Fallout

The next morning, Mae woke with a sense of foreboding, her body still warm from the memory of Michael's touch but her mind racing with anxiety about what the day would bring. She lay there for a moment, tangled in her sheets, replaying their passionate encounter in the greenhouse. It had been raw, intense, everything she needed — a moment of connection in a sea of chaos. But now, as the sun filtered through the thin curtains, reality came rushing back. The rumor she had spread was taking root, and she had no idea what the consequences would be.

She finally forced herself out of bed, quickly getting dressed, her hands shaking slightly as she buttoned her shirt. She needed to know what was happening, needed to find out if her plan had worked, if the administration had taken the bait. She couldn't help but feel a mix of hope and dread as she made her way across campus, every glance around her filled with paranoia.

When she reached the main courtyard, she saw small groups of students gathered, whispering among themselves. She caught snippets of their conversations — mentions of the investigation, murmurs of doubt about its legitimacy. She felt a small spark of satisfaction. It seemed her rumor was spreading, the seed of doubt she had planted starting to grow.

But then, she heard something else, something that made her blood run cold.

"I heard they're going to make an example out of him," a girl whispered to her friend. "Professor Arden... they want him gone."

Mae felt her stomach twist, a wave of nausea crashing over her. She quickly moved closer, straining to hear more.

"Yeah, I heard the dean's furious," the other girl replied. "They're saying he crossed a line, that he's been seen with students... alone. They're looking for any reason to fire him."

Mae's heart pounded in her chest, her mind spinning. She needed to find Jess, needed to know what was going on behind closed doors. She turned and headed toward the library, hoping to find her there, hoping for some clarity.

Jess was sitting in their usual spot, her face buried in a textbook, but her expression was tense, her fingers tapping nervously on the table. Mae hurried over, sliding into the seat across from her.

"Jess," she whispered urgently. "What's happening? What did you hear?"

Jess looked up, her eyes wide with concern. "It's bad, Mae," she replied, her voice low. "The meeting yesterday... it didn't go well. They're talking about pushing Michael out, saying he's a liability. They want to avoid a scandal, and they think getting rid of him is the easiest way."

Mae felt a wave of panic rise in her chest. "But what about the rumor?" she asked. "Didn't that help?"

Jess nodded, but her expression remained grim. "It helped a little," she admitted. "It's caused some doubt, some confusion. But the dean is determined, and there are a few faculty members who want to see Michael gone. They think he's a threat to the university's reputation."

"What can we do?" Mae whispered, her voice trembling. "We can't just let them do this."

Jess bit her lip, thinking. "I've been talking to my contact," she said slowly. "They told me there's going to be another meeting soon — today, actually. This one is to discuss the formal recommendation for his suspension. If we can get some of the faculty to speak up in his defense, it might sway things."

Mae nodded, a sense of determination settling over her. "I'll talk to some people," she said. "There are a few professors who like Michael, who respect him. Maybe they'll listen."

Jess reached out, squeezing Mae's hand. "Be careful," she urged. "You're already on their radar. Don't give them any more reason to come after you."

Mae nodded, feeling a tightness in her chest. "I will," she promised. "But I can't just sit back and do nothing."

The hours ticked by with agonizing slowness as Mae moved through campus, trying to rally support for Michael. She approached a few professors she knew, those who had always been friendly with Michael, carefully choosing her words, planting the idea that the investigation was unjust, that it was motivated by personal vendettas rather than any real misconduct.

She could see some of them listening, nodding slowly, their expressions thoughtful. But she could also sense the doubt in their eyes, the fear of being dragged into something messy, something that could damage their own standing. She knew it was a long shot, but she had to try.

By the afternoon, she felt exhausted, her nerves frayed, but she knew she couldn't give up. She needed to see Michael, needed to hear his voice, to feel his touch, to remind herself why they were fighting so hard.

She sent another discreet message, a note slipped under his door: "Meet me at the old greenhouse. Midnight."

That night, Mae waited in the greenhouse, her heart racing with anticipation and fear. The space was dark, the only light coming from the slivers of moonlight filtering through the cracked *glass. She paced nervously, her breath coming in short, shallow bursts.*

When Michael finally appeared, she rushed to him, wrapping her arms around his neck, pulling him close. "Michael," she whispered, her voice filled with urgency. "They're going to try to push you out. I've been talking to people, trying to get support, but I don't know if it's enough."

Michael held her tight, his hands stroking her back, his face buried in her hair. "I know," he murmured softly. "I've heard the same. But Mae... we have to be careful. If they find out we're meeting like this, it will only make things worse."

"I don't care," she whispered fiercely, pulling back to look into his eyes. "I don't care about the risks. I just need you. I need to feel you, Michael."

His eyes softened, and he cupped her face in his hands, his thumbs brushing her cheeks. "Mae," he murmured, his voice thick with emotion, "I need you too... more than anything."

He kissed her then, deeply, his lips hungry and desperate against hers. Mae felt the fire ignite between them again, felt the tension of the day melt away under the heat of his touch. His hands moved to her waist, pulling her closer, his body pressing against hers.

She moaned softly, her hands sliding under his shirt, feeling the warmth of his skin, the hard muscles of his back. "Michael," she breathed, her voice trembling with need, "make me forget... make me forget everything."

He groaned, his lips moving to her neck, kissing a trail down to her collarbone, his hands roaming her body with a rough, insistent urgency. "I will," he promised, his voice low and husky. "I'll make you forget everything but us."

He lifted her onto the old table, his body pressing against hers, his hands sliding up her thighs, pushing her skirt higher. She gasped, feeling the cool air against her skin, the heat of his body between her legs. "Michael," she whispered, her breath catching in her throat, "please... I need you."

He smiled against her lips, a wicked, satisfied smile. "I'm here," he murmured, his fingers finding the edge of her panties, sliding them down slowly, teasingly. "I'm not going anywhere."

She felt her body respond to his touch, felt the heat pooling low in her belly, her breath coming in short, desperate gasps. "Please," she whispered again, her hands gripping his shoulders, pulling him closer. "Now."

Michael didn't hesitate. He kissed her deeply, his hands moving with purpose, his body pressing hers into the table. Mae felt herself let go, giving in to the sensations coursing through her, her body arching against his, needing more, wanting everything.

He moved against her, his body firm and insistent, his hands gripping her hips, guiding her movements, their rhythm building faster, more urgent. Mae felt herself spiraling, her body trembling, her breath catching in her throat as she reached for him, holding on as if he were the only solid thing in a world spinning out of control.

They moved together in perfect sync, each thrust bringing them closer to the edge. She could feel the tension building inside her, could feel the pressure mounting, like a storm ready to break. Her nails dug into his back, her head falling back, a moan escaping her lips.

"Yes, Mae," Michael murmured, his voice rough with desire. "Let go... let go for me."

His words sent a shockwave through her, and she felt herself shatter, her body convulsing as a wave of pleasure crashed over her. She cried out, her voice a mix of ecstasy and relief, her body trembling with the force of her climax.

Michael followed her over the edge, his body tensing, his grip tightening on her hips as he found his own release, a deep, satisfied groan rumbling in his chest. They held onto each other, their bodies entwined, their breaths mingling in the cool night air.

They stayed like that for a long time, wrapped in each other's arms, their bodies still humming with the aftershocks of their passion. Mae rested her head against his chest, her eyes closed, listening to the steady rhythm of his heartbeat. It was a sound that grounded her, made her feel safe, even amidst the chaos that surrounded them.

For a moment, the world outside seemed to fade away, the threats and the whispers, the fear of discovery — none of it mattered. Here, in his arms, she felt complete, whole. She felt the warmth of his skin, the rise and fall of his chest, and she allowed herself to believe, just for a moment, that everything would be okay.

Michael's fingers stroked her hair softly, his other hand still holding her close. "I wish we could stay like this forever," he murmured, his voice filled with a quiet longing.

"Me too," Mae whispered, her voice barely audible. "But we can't, can we?"

He sighed, his grip tightening around her as if he could somehow shield her from the world. "No," he admitted softly. "Not yet, anyway. But we'll find a way, Mae. I swear, we'll find a way to make this work."

Mae looked up at him, her eyes searching his, finding the determination there, the fierce protectiveness that made her heart ache with love. "I believe you," she said, her voice filled with conviction. "We'll get through this. Together."

He smiled, a small, tender smile that made her heart flutter. "Together," he echoed, his thumb brushing over her cheek. "No matter what."

They stood there for a few more minutes, holding each other in the dim light of the greenhouse, their breaths slowing, their bodies still pressed close. But the reality of their situation crept back in, the danger and the uncertainty pressing down on them like a weight.

Michael finally pulled back slightly, his expression turning serious. "I have to be careful from now on," he said quietly. "If they're really looking for any excuse to push me out, I can't afford to make any mistakes."

Mae nodded, understanding. "I know," she replied. "And I'll do whatever I can to help. I'll keep talking to people, trying to turn them to our side."

Michael looked at her, his eyes filled with a mix of admiration and concern. "Just... promise me you'll be careful, Mae," he said, his voice low. "I couldn't bear it if something happened to you because of this."

She smiled softly, reaching up to brush a strand of hair from his face. "I promise," she whispered. "But I won't just stand by and let them take you away from me."

He kissed her again, a slow, lingering kiss that spoke of all the things they couldn't say, all the fears and hopes and dreams they shared. When they finally pulled apart, he rested his forehead against hers, his breath warm against her skin.

"I should go," he murmured reluctantly. "Before anyone notices I'm gone."

Mae nodded, her heart sinking at the thought of him leaving, but knowing he was right. "I'll see you soon?" she asked, her voice tinged with both hope and anxiety.

He smiled, a small, reassuring smile. "Soon," he promised. "We'll find a way to be together. Always."

She watched as he slipped out into the night, disappearing into the shadows. Mae stood there for a moment longer, her heart racing, her mind spinning with everything that had happened, everything that was still to come. She took a deep breath, steadying herself. She had to be strong. For him. For them.

Turning, she left the greenhouse, slipping quietly through the darkened campus, her steps light and quick. She knew the risks, knew they were growing with every day, but she also knew that she couldn't give up now. She wouldn't give up on Michael, wouldn't give up on what they had. Not when they had fought so hard, come so far.

The next day, the atmosphere on campus felt even more charged, the tension almost palpable. Mae kept her head down, moving quickly through the halls, listening closely to the snippets of conversation around her.

She heard more rumors, more speculation — that the administration was close to making a decision, that Michael's fate hung in the balance. She felt her stomach twist with fear, but she pushed it down, refusing to let it take hold. She had to stay focused, had to keep fighting.

She made her way to the small coffee shop near the east gate, a place where students and faculty often gathered to talk. She needed to find allies, needed to keep the pressure on the administration, to make them think twice about pushing Michael out.

As she entered, she spotted a familiar face — Professor Hall, one of the few faculty members who had always been kind to Michael, who had always seemed to respect him. Mae hesitated for a moment, then moved toward her, her heart pounding.

"Professor Hall," she greeted, trying to keep her voice steady, "do you have a minute?"

The older woman looked up, her expression curious but open. "Mae," she said with a small smile. "Of course. What can I do for you?"

Mae took a deep breath, steeling herself. "I wanted to talk to you about Michael," she began carefully. "About what's happening. I know there are a lot of rumors, but I think the administration is making a mistake. He's a good professor, a good man, and I don't think it's fair what they're doing."

Professor Hall nodded slowly, her expression thoughtful. "I've heard some things," she admitted. "And I agree, it does seem... heavy-handed. But there's a lot of pressure right now, a lot of people asking questions."

"I know," Mae replied quickly. "But that's why we need people like you to speak up, to stand up for him. If they hear it from respected faculty, they might listen. They might reconsider."

The professor considered her words, her eyes narrowing slightly. "You care about him a great deal, don't you?" she asked gently.

Mae felt a blush rise to her cheeks, but she nodded. "I do," she confessed quietly. "He's a good man, and he doesn't deserve this."

Professor Hall smiled softly, a knowing look in her eyes. "Alright, Mae," she said after a moment. "I'll see what I can do.

But you should be careful, too. This is a delicate situation, and you don't want to make yourself a target."

"I understand," Mae replied, a flicker of hope igniting in her chest. "Thank you, Professor Hall. I appreciate it more than you know."

The professor nodded, giving her a reassuring pat on the arm. "Take care, Mae," she said softly. "And don't lose hope."

Mae left the coffee shop feeling a little lighter, a little more determined. She knew they still had a long way to go, but she also knew they weren't alone. There were people who believed in Michael, who believed in them, and she had to hold on to that.

That evening, as Mae walked back to her dorm, she felt her phone buzz in her pocket. She quickly pulled it out, her heart leaping when she saw Michael's name on the screen.

Michael: *Meet me. Tonight. Usual place. Urgent.*

Mae's heart fluttered as she quickly typed back a reply.

Mae: *I'll be there.*

She felt a surge of anticipation, a mix of fear and hope. She didn't know what Michael wanted to tell her, but she knew it was important. She hurried to her room, quickly changing into something warmer, her mind spinning with possibilities.

And as she made her way through the darkened campus, heading once again to the old greenhouse, she felt a flicker of determination in her chest. Whatever came next, whatever they faced, she knew they would face it together. And for now, that was enough.

Chapter 16: The Countdown Begins

Mae arrived at the old greenhouse, her breath visible in the cool night air. Her heart raced, a mix of fear and anticipation thrumming in her veins. She glanced around, her eyes adjusting to the darkness, the familiar shapes of broken tables and overgrown plants looming around her. She waited, listening for the sound of footsteps, every nerve in her body on edge.

And then, she heard him — the soft crunch of gravel under his feet, the whisper of his breath in the quiet night. Michael stepped into the greenhouse, his expression tense, his eyes dark with worry. He moved quickly to her, his hands immediately finding her arms, pulling her close.

"Mae," he whispered urgently, his voice rough with emotion. "I'm glad you came."

"Of course," she replied softly, her fingers brushing his cheek, feeling the roughness of his stubble. "What's going on? What did you find out?"

Michael took a deep breath, his hands gripping her shoulders, his gaze intense. "Things are worse than we thought," he said quietly. "The administration isn't just considering my suspension. They've already decided to push for it. They're convening a special meeting with the board tomorrow morning to finalize everything."

Mae's heart dropped, fear surging through her. "Tomorrow morning?" she echoed, her voice trembling. "That soon?"

He nodded, his expression grim. "Yes. They want to do it quickly, to avoid any more speculation or backlash. They think if they act fast, they can control the narrative, keep things from spiraling further."

Mae felt a wave of panic, her mind spinning. "What can we do?" she asked desperately. "Is there any way to stop them?"

Michael hesitated, his brow furrowing. "I've been thinking," he began slowly, "there might be one last chance to turn this around. But it's risky."

"Tell me," Mae urged, her hands gripping his arms. "I'll do anything, Michael. Anything to help."

He took a deep breath, his eyes searching hers. "We need to get ahead of this," he explained. "If we can make a public statement — something that casts doubt on the administration's motives — we might be able to sway enough people to make them reconsider. But it means going public, Mae. It means exposing ourselves."

Mae felt her heart skip a beat. "Public?" she whispered, the word heavy in her mouth. "You mean... tell everyone about us?"

Michael nodded slowly, his expression serious. "Yes," he replied. "It's a gamble, but it might be our only chance. If we can frame this as a fight against an unfair system, against a witch hunt, we might be able to get the students, even some faculty, on our side. But it will mean facing whatever comes head-on."

Mae swallowed hard, the weight of his words settling over her. "And what if it doesn't work?" she asked quietly. "What if they still push you out?"

Michael sighed, his grip on her tightening. "Then we deal with it," he said softly. "But at least we'll know we tried everything. At least we won't have gone down without a fight."

Mae looked up at him, her eyes filled with determination. "I'll do it," she said firmly. "I'll stand with you, Michael. Whatever happens, I'm not going to hide anymore."

He smiled, a small, sad smile that made her heart ache. "I knew you would," he murmured, his fingers brushing her hair back. "But we need to be smart about this. We need to plan."

"What do you suggest?" Mae asked, her mind racing with possibilities.

"We hold a press conference," Michael replied. "We get a few sympathetic students, maybe a professor or two, to stand with us. We make our case — that this is about more than just us, that it's about fairness, about the right to be heard. If we can create enough doubt, enough noise, they might back off."

Mae nodded, her fear tempered by a flicker of hope. "Okay," she agreed. "But we'll need to move fast. We don't have much time."

Michael leaned in, kissing her softly, his lips lingering on hers. "I know," he whispered against her mouth. "But we're in this together, Mae. We'll make them listen."

She kissed him back, a fierce determination filling her. "Together," she echoed, her voice strong.

The next morning, the campus was buzzing with activity. Mae and Michael had spent the night contacting allies, gathering support, and preparing for what would come next. They had managed to secure a small group of students and faculty who were willing to stand with them, who believed in their cause.

Mae felt a strange mix of fear and excitement as she made her way to the main courtyard, where they had decided to hold the press conference. Her heart pounded in her chest, her palms damp with sweat. She knew this was their last chance, their final stand.

Michael was already there, talking quietly with a few professors who had agreed to speak on their behalf. He looked up *as she approached, his face lighting up with a mixture of relief and determination.*

"Mae," he greeted, his hand reaching out to hers. "Are you ready for this?"

She nodded, squeezing his hand tightly. "As ready as I'll ever be," she replied, her voice steady despite the fear swirling in her stomach.

They moved to the center of the courtyard, where a small crowd had already gathered, students and faculty murmuring among themselves, curious about what was happening. Mae felt her heart race as she looked out over the sea of faces, some supportive, others skeptical, all of them watching.

Michael stepped forward, clearing his throat, his voice carrying over the crowd. "Thank you all for coming," he began, his tone calm but strong. "I know there have been a lot of rumors, a lot of speculation about what's been happening. I want to take this opportunity to set the record straight."

The crowd quieted, all eyes on him. Mae stood beside him, her heart pounding, her breath shallow. She felt his hand squeeze hers, a small gesture of reassurance, and she took a deep breath, preparing herself for what was to come.

"Yes, Mae and I are involved," Michael continued, his voice steady. "We are in a relationship. But this isn't about that. This is about more than just us. This is about fairness, about the right to be treated with respect, about standing up against a system that uses its power to silence dissent."

There were murmurs in the crowd, a mix of surprise and curiosity. Mae felt a surge of adrenaline, a spark of hope that maybe, just maybe, they could turn this around.

"The administration wants to make an example of us," Michael went on, his gaze sweeping over the crowd. "They want to push me out, to silence me because I refuse to conform to their expectations. But we won't be silenced. We won't be intimidated."

Mae stepped forward, her voice trembling but strong. "We're asking for your support," she said, her eyes scanning the faces before her. "We're asking you to stand with us, to demand fairness, to demand a system that respects all of us, students and faculty alike."

There was a pause, a moment of tension, and then a few students began to clap, hesitantly at first, then louder, more confident. The sound grew, spreading through the crowd, and Mae felt a flicker of hope ignite in her chest.

Professor Hall stepped forward, raising her voice above the applause. "I stand with Michael and Mae," she declared firmly. "This is about more than just them. This is about ensuring our campus remains a place where we can speak our minds, where we can challenge the status quo without fear of reprisal."

The crowd erupted into applause, and Mae felt tears sting her eyes, a wave of emotion crashing over her. She looked up at Michael, who was smiling, a mixture of pride and relief on his face.

But then, from the back of the crowd, a voice cut through the noise, sharp and accusatory. "This is a distraction!" someone shouted. "They're just trying to save themselves!"

Mae felt her heart sink, her body tensing. She saw Tom step forward, his face twisted with anger. "They're manipulating you!" he yelled, pointing at them. "This is just a ploy to cover up what they've done!"

The crowd quieted, uncertainty rippling through the air. Mae felt panic rising, but she forced herself to stay calm. She looked at Michael, who nodded slightly, his eyes telling her to hold steady.

Michael raised his hand, signaling for calm. "Tom," he said evenly, "we're not here to manipulate anyone. We're here to tell the truth. If you have something to say, go ahead. But we ask that you listen to what we have to say as well."

Tom sneered, his eyes narrowing. "The truth?" he spat. "The truth is, you're using your position to take advantage of a student, and now you're trying to make it look like you're the victim!"

The crowd murmured, some nodding, others shaking their heads. Mae felt her stomach twist, fear clawing at her insides. But she stepped forward, her voice steady, clear.

"I am not a victim," she said loudly, her gaze locking onto Tom's. "I am here because I choose to be. Because I believe in Michael, in what we have. And because I believe in the right to stand up for ourselves, for our love, without fear of persecution."

There was a silence, a tense moment where everything hung in the balance. Mae felt her heart pounding, her hands shaking. She glanced at Michael, who gave her a small, encouraging smile, and she felt a surge of strength.

The crowd began to murmur again, some in support, others still uncertain. Mae could see the doubt, the conflict in their faces, and she knew they were on the edge, that this was their moment to sway them, to turn the tide.

Michael stepped closer to her, his hand finding hers, and together, they faced the crowd, their heads held high, their hearts beating as one. They had come too far, fought too hard, to back down now.

"*This is our truth,*" *Michael said firmly, his voice strong. "And we will not be silenced.*"

The applause began to swell again, louder this time, and Mae felt a spark of hope ignite in her chest. They weren't alone. Not anymore.

Chapter 17: The Fallout of Defiance

The energy on campus was electric in the wake of the press conference. Mae could feel it in the air, a palpable tension buzzing around her as she walked through the halls. Some students glanced at her with curiosity, others with thinly veiled judgment, but a few nodded or smiled in quiet support. She held her head high, determined not to let the scrutiny wear her down. But inside, she was a storm of emotions — fear, hope, defiance, and a gnawing anxiety about what would come next.

She knew they had made an impact, but she wasn't sure if it was enough. Tom's accusations still hung in the air like a dark cloud, and she worried that his words might sway some of the faculty, that they might see her and Michael's defiance as further proof of their guilt. She had done everything she could to help turn the tide, but now, she had to wait and see how it all played out.

Mae found herself heading toward the small, secluded garden behind the arts building, a quiet place she often went to think. She needed a moment to clear her head, to gather her thoughts. As she turned the corner, she spotted Jess sitting on a bench, her face tense, her eyes scanning the path ahead.

"Mae," Jess called out softly, motioning for her to join her. "Over here."

Mae hurried over, her heart racing. "Jess, what's going on?" she asked urgently. "Have you heard anything?"

Jess nodded, her expression serious. "I've been talking to some of the faculty," she replied, her voice low. "There's definitely a lot of division. Some are starting to question the administration's motives, especially after what you and Michael said today. But others... they're still on the fence. Tom's words made an impact."

Mae felt a knot of anxiety tighten in her stomach. "What do you think?" she asked. "Do we have a chance?"

Jess hesitated, then nodded. "I think so," she said slowly. "But it's going to be close. There's a meeting happening later this afternoon, a final decision meeting. If we can get enough people on our side, we might be able to sway the vote. But it's going to take more than just words."

"What do you mean?" Mae asked, her brow furrowing.

"I mean," Jess replied, her voice urgent, "we need more leverage. Something concrete, something that forces them to rethink. Right now, they're weighing their options, but they need a push."

Mae bit her lip, thinking. "What kind of leverage?" she asked slowly.

Jess glanced around, then leaned in closer. "I've been doing some digging," she whispered. "There are rumors that one of the board members — Dean Caldwell, specifically — has some skeletons in her closet. Something about an affair with a former student, something that was hushed up. If we can find proof, if we can expose it... it might be enough to force them to back off."

Mae's eyes widened. "Are you sure?" she whispered. "That's... that's risky, Jess."

Jess nodded. "I know," she said. "But if it's true, it could be the leverage we need. They won't want to risk a scandal of their own. They'll have to back down."

Mae felt a surge of adrenaline, her mind racing. "How do we find proof?" she asked. "Do you have any idea where to start?"

Jess hesitated, then pulled out her phone, showing Mae a series of messages. "I've been talking to a former student," she explained. "Someone who was here a few years ago. They hinted that there were some emails, some documents that were buried. If we can find them, we might have what we need."

Mae stared at the screen, her heart pounding. "Okay," she said finally. "Let's do it. How do we get those emails?"

Jess looked around, making sure no one was listening. "We need to access the administration's records," she replied. "And I think I know someone who can help."

Later that afternoon, Mae found herself standing outside the IT office, her nerves buzzing with a mix of fear and determination. Jess had introduced her to a friend of hers, Alex, a tech-savvy student who worked part-time in the IT department. He had agreed to help, but Mae knew they were walking a fine line. One wrong move, and everything could blow up in their faces.

Alex emerged from the office, a lanky young man with a quick smile and bright eyes. "Hey, Mae," he greeted, his voice hushed. "Jess filled me in. I can help, but this isn't going to be easy."

"I understand," Mae replied, trying to keep her voice steady. "What do we need to do?"

Alex glanced around, then motioned for her to follow him. "Come on," he said. "I've got access to some of the old servers, but we need to be quick. If they catch us snooping around, we're done."

Mae nodded, following him into a small, dimly lit room filled with computer screens and cables. Alex sat down at one of the terminals, his fingers flying over the keyboard. "I'll need a few minutes to get into the right directories," he explained, his voice calm and focused. "Just keep an eye on the door."

Mae stood by the entrance, her heart racing, her eyes darting back and forth. Every sound, every footstep in the hallway made her jump, her nerves stretched taut. She glanced back at Alex, watching as he worked, his face illuminated by the glow of the screen.

"Got it," Alex muttered after a few tense minutes. "I'm in. Now, let's see if I can find those emails."

Mae held her breath, her heart pounding in her chest. She watched as Alex navigated through files, his eyes scanning the screen with quick, practiced movements. After a few moments, he let out a low whistle.

"Bingo," he whispered, a grin spreading across his face. "I found something. A folder with some old correspondence... and it looks like there's something here about Dean Caldwell."

"Open it," Mae urged, her voice tight with anticipation.

Alex clicked on the folder, his eyes widening as he read the contents. "Holy shit," he murmured. "There's definitely something here. Emails between Caldwell and a former student... and they're not exactly professional."

Mae's heart leapt. "Can you download them?" she asked quickly. "We need to have something to show."

Alex nodded, his fingers moving quickly over the keyboard. "I'm on it," he replied. "But we need to move fast. If anyone catches on that we're accessing these files, we're screwed."

He transferred the files to a flash drive, his movements swift and efficient. "Got it," he said finally, pulling the drive from the computer. "Let's get out of here."

Mae nodded, feeling a rush of adrenaline. "Thank you," she whispered as they slipped out of the room. "This could change everything."

"Just be careful," Alex warned. "And make sure you use this wisely."

"I will," Mae promised, clutching the drive tightly in her hand. "We have to."

By late afternoon, the campus was abuzz with speculation. Mae knew they didn't have much time. The meeting was fast approaching, and they needed to act before the board made its final decision.

She hurried to meet Michael near the faculty building, her heart racing with a mix of fear and excitement. He was waiting for her, his expression tense, his eyes filled with concern.

"Mae," he greeted, his voice low. "What did you find?"

Mae held up the flash drive, a small smile tugging at her lips. "Leverage," she replied. "Proof that Dean Caldwell isn't exactly the paragon of virtue she claims to be."

Michael's eyes widened, a mix of surprise and admiration. "You did it," he murmured. "But Mae... this is risky. Are you sure about this?"

"We don't have a choice," she said firmly. "If we don't use this, they'll push you out, and we'll lose everything. We have to fight back."

He nodded slowly, his hand reaching out to cup her face. "I trust you," he whispered. "I trust us."

Mae felt a surge of emotion, her heart swelling with love and determination. "Then let's do this," she said, her voice steady. "Let's make our move."

They moved quickly, heading to the administration building where the meeting was about to begin. Mae's heart pounded in her chest as they approached the heavy wooden doors, the tension in the air thick and suffocating.

Michael knocked, and after a moment, the door opened, revealing a surprised-looking Dean Caldwell. Her expression quickly turned to a frown. "What are you doing here?" she demanded, her voice cold.

"We need to talk," Michael said firmly. "Before you make any decisions."

Dean Caldwell crossed her arms, her gaze hard. "We have nothing to discuss," she snapped. "You've made your choices, and now you'll face the consequences."

"I think you'll want to hear this," Mae interjected, holding up the flash drive. "Before you make any hasty decisions."

Dean Caldwell's eyes flicked to the drive, a flash of worry crossing her face. "What is that?" she asked, her voice suddenly wary.

"Evidence," Michael replied calmly. "Evidence that you might not want to come to light. Evidence that shows you're not exactly impartial in this matter."

The dean's face paled, her hands clenching at her sides. "You're bluffing," she hissed. "You have nothing."

"Would you like to see for yourself?" Mae challenged, stepping forward, her voice steady. "Or would you rather reconsider your position before we make this public?"

There was a tense silence, the weight of the moment pressing down on them like a heavy cloud. Mae held her breath, waiting, hoping. She could see the fear in Dean Caldwell's eyes, the uncertainty, the calculation.

Finally, the dean took a deep breath, her expression hardening. "Fine," she said tightly. "Come inside. We'll hear what you have to say."

Mae felt a rush of relief and fear as they stepped into the room, the eyes of the board members turning toward them. This was it. Their last chance. The moment that would decide everything.

Michael squeezed her hand, a small, reassuring gesture, and she looked up at him, finding strength in his gaze.

"Let's do this," he whispered.

Chapter 18: The Gamble

The room was filled with a thick tension, so heavy it felt like Mae could cut through it with a knife. She stood beside Michael, her hand still in his, her heart racing as the board members stared at them with a mix of curiosity, suspicion, and unease. She could feel her pulse pounding in her ears, the adrenaline coursing through her veins, but she held her ground, refusing to show any fear.

Dean Caldwell sat at the head of the long table, her face pale and tight, her eyes flicking back and forth between Mae, Michael, and the flash drive that Mae held in her hand. "What is this all about?" she demanded, her voice sharp but with an edge of uncertainty that didn't go unnoticed.

"It's about fairness," Michael replied calmly, his voice steady, though Mae could feel the tension in his grip. "It's about transparency. You've accused me of misconduct without evidence. Meanwhile, it seems there may be evidence of misconduct from within your own administration."

Mae watched the reactions of the board members closely. She saw a few raise their eyebrows, some shift in their seats, a flicker of uncertainty in their eyes. They hadn't expected this. That was a good sign.

Dean Caldwell's jaw clenched, her hands gripping the edge of the table. "You're bluffing," she hissed, though Mae could hear the tremor in her voice. "You think you can intimidate me with baseless threats?"

Mae stepped forward, her voice clear and confident. "It's not a threat, Dean Caldwell," she said. "It's a promise. We have evidence

— emails, correspondence — that suggest you've engaged in behavior not so different from what you're accusing Michael of. And we're prepared to make this public if necessary."

There was a murmur among the board members, a ripple of discomfort that spread through the room. Mae could see the dean's facade starting to crack, a flicker of fear crossing her face.

One of the board members, a woman with sharp features and a skeptical gaze, leaned forward. "Is this true, Dean Caldwell?" she asked pointedly. "Is there any basis to what they're saying?"

The dean's eyes darted around the room, her face tightening. "Of course not," she snapped. "This is a desperate attempt to deflect attention from their own wrongdoing."

"Then you won't mind if we share this with the press?" Michael interjected, his tone calm but firm. "After all, if it's nothing, there's nothing to hide."

Dean Caldwell's face flushed, her hands clenching tighter. "You wouldn't dare," she spat. "This could ruin you."

"Maybe," Michael replied, his gaze steady, "but it could also ruin you. And we're willing to take that chance."

The board members exchanged uneasy glances, and Mae could feel the shift in the room, the balance of power slowly tipping. They had them on the defensive now, and they needed to press their advantage.

Mae took a deep breath, stepping forward again. "All we're asking for is a fair hearing," she said, her voice strong and unwavering. "If you're going to investigate Michael, then you should be willing to investigate all potential misconduct, including your own. If not, then you have no right to judge him."

There was a tense silence, the air thick with anticipation. Finally, the board member with the sharp features spoke again.

"Dean Caldwell," she said slowly, "if there's any truth to these claims, we need to address them. The integrity of this institution depends on it."

The dean's face was a mask of fury, but Mae could see the fear in her eyes, the realization that her options were dwindling. "This is absurd," she muttered, but there was no conviction in her voice, only desperation.

"Perhaps," the board member continued, "we should take some time to review the evidence before making any decisions. If there's any question of impropriety, it must be dealt with appropriately."

Mae felt a surge of hope, her heart leaping in her chest. She glanced at Michael, who gave her a small, encouraging nod. They were getting through. They were being heard.

Dean Caldwell glared at Mae and Michael, her eyes cold and hard. "You're playing a dangerous game," she whispered fiercely. "You think you've won, but you have no idea what you're up against."

"Maybe," Mae replied softly, her voice steady, "but we're not afraid of you. Not anymore."

The dean's eyes narrowed, her lips curling into a sneer. "Very well," she said through gritted teeth. "We will reconvene tomorrow morning to review this... so-called evidence. But don't think for a moment that this is over."

The board members began to murmur among themselves, some nodding in agreement, others looking uncomfortable. Mae could feel the tension in the room shift, the balance of power tilting further in their favor. They had bought themselves some time, and now, they needed to use it wisely.

Michael turned to Mae, his expression a mix of relief and determination. "Let's go," he whispered, squeezing her hand. "We've done all we can for now."

Mae nodded, feeling a wave of exhaustion wash over her. She followed him out of the room, the door closing behind them with a heavy thud. They walked quickly down the hall, their footsteps echoing in the empty corridor.

When they were finally outside, Michael pulled her into his arms, holding her tight. "You were amazing," he murmured against her hair. "I couldn't have done this without you."

Mae felt a rush of warmth, a swell of pride in her chest. "We're in this together," she whispered, leaning into him. "No matter what happens."

He kissed her softly, a slow, tender kiss that made her heart flutter, that made the world around them fade away. "I love you," he breathed against her lips. "I love you so damn much."

"I love you too," she whispered back, her hands resting on his chest, feeling the steady beat of his heart under her palms. "And we're going to get through this. Together."

They stood there for a long moment, wrapped in each other's arms, drawing strength from their connection. The night air was cool and crisp, a gentle breeze rustling the leaves around them. For a moment, everything felt still, calm, as if the universe was holding its breath, waiting to see what would come next.

"We need to be ready for tomorrow," Michael said finally, pulling back slightly but still holding her close. "We need to make sure we have everything we need, every piece of evidence, every argument. We can't leave anything to chance."

"I know," Mae agreed, her mind already racing with plans. "I'll talk to Alex, see if there's anything else we can find. Maybe we

can get some more information, something that strengthens our case."

Michael nodded, his eyes filled with determination. "And I'll speak to a few more faculty members, see if we can get more support. We're going to need everyone we can get."

"We'll do this," Mae said, her voice filled with conviction. "We'll make them listen."

He smiled, a small, fierce smile that made her heart swell. "Yes," he agreed. "We will."

The next morning dawned with a heavy, overcast sky, a thick blanket of gray clouds hanging low over the campus. Mae felt the weight of the day pressing down on her as she made her way to the administration building, her stomach churning with nerves. She knew this was it, their last chance to turn things around.

She met Michael outside, his face tense but focused, his eyes sharp with determination. "Are you ready?" he asked, his voice steady but soft.

"As ready as I'll ever be," Mae replied, squeezing his hand. "Let's do this."

They walked together into the building, heading for the meeting room where the board was already gathered. The atmosphere was thick with tension, the air heavy with anticipation. Mae could feel the eyes of the board members on them as they entered, could feel the weight of their scrutiny, their judgment.

Dean Caldwell sat at the head of the table, her face a mask of cold determination. She looked up as they approached, her eyes narrowing slightly. "You have one chance to present your... evidence," she said icily. "Make it quick."

Michael nodded, his hand steady on Mae's back. "We'll be brief," he replied. "But we believe it's important that everyone sees the truth."

He handed the flash drive to one of the board members, who plugged it into a laptop connected to a projector. The room was silent, every eye on the screen as the files opened, the emails appearing in stark black and white.

There were gasps, murmurs of shock and disbelief as the content of the emails became clear — the flirtatious language, the suggestions of meetings, the clear implications of an inappropriate relationship between Dean Caldwell and a former student.

Dean Caldwell's face went white, her hands clenched into fists on the table. "This is... this is private," she stammered, her voice shaking with anger. "This has nothing to do with this case!"

"It has everything to do with this case," Michael countered firmly. "If you're going to accuse me of misconduct, you need to be held to the same standard. This is about fairness, about transparency. We deserve that much."

The room was silent, every eye on Dean Caldwell, every face filled with a mix of shock and uncertainty. Mae felt her heart pounding, her breath catching in her throat. This was it. The moment of truth.

The board member with the sharp features spoke up again, her voice calm but firm. "I think," she said slowly, "that we need to take a step back and review all the facts, all the evidence, before making any final decisions. It's clear that there are questions that need answers."

Dean Caldwell's face was a mask of fury, but she nodded, her lips pressed into a thin line. "Very well," she said tightly. "We will reconvene in a week to discuss this further."

Mae felt a surge of relief, her knees almost buckling with the force of it. They had done it. They had bought themselves more time.

Michael squeezed her hand, a small smile of triumph on his lips. "We're not done yet," he whispered, "but we've taken a big step."

"Yes," Mae agreed, her voice filled with quiet determination. "And we're not going to stop. Not until we win."

Chapter 19: Lines in the Sand

The days following the meeting felt like a blur. Mae moved through campus with a strange sense of urgency and anxiety, her mind constantly racing with thoughts of what was to come. She knew they had bought themselves time, but she also knew it was only temporary. The board would reconvene in a week, and the stakes were higher than ever. She and Michael needed to be ready for whatever came next.

She could feel the shift in the air around her. The campus was alive with rumors, whispers that seemed to follow her wherever she went. Some students looked at her with newfound curiosity, some with sympathy, others with suspicion. It was like being caught in the eye of a storm, where everything felt precarious, on the verge of collapse.

Mae decided to keep herself busy. She couldn't afford to dwell on the uncertainty, not when there was still so much to do. She had meetings to attend, people to speak with, plans to make. She had promised Michael she would fight with him, and that was exactly what she intended to do.

That afternoon, she found herself in the student union, sitting with Jess and a few other students who had been vocal in their support of her and Michael. They were huddled around a small table, their voices hushed as they discussed the events of the past few days.

"We need to keep the pressure on," Jess was saying, her eyes sharp with determination. "We can't let the administration think we're backing down. We need more students to speak up, more faculty to question the motives behind this investigation."

Mae nodded in agreement. "We need to make it clear that this isn't just about Michael and me," she added. "It's about the culture of fear and control they're trying to enforce. If we can show that this investigation is a symptom of a larger problem, we might have a chance."

One of the other students, a tall girl with glasses, leaned forward. "But how do we do that?" she asked. "How do we get people to see that it's not just about your relationship, but about the way the administration is handling it?"

Mae took a deep breath, considering her words carefully. "We need to frame this as a broader fight for student rights," she explained. "We need to show that if they can come after us, they can come after anyone. We need to make it personal for everyone."

Jess nodded, her expression thoughtful. "We could organize a protest," she suggested. "Something that draws attention, that makes a statement. Maybe a sit-in at the administration building?"

Mae felt a spark of excitement. "That could work," she agreed. "If we get enough people involved, it could force them to listen. It could show that we're not afraid to stand up for ourselves."

"And we should get the media involved," another student chimed in, a young man with a bright smile. "If we can get local reporters to cover it, the administration won't be able to ignore us."

"Exactly," Mae said, her heart racing with a mix of fear and hope. "We need to make this as public as possible. We need to shine a light on what's happening here."

The group continued to brainstorm, their voices growing louder, more confident. Mae felt a sense of solidarity growing among them, a shared purpose that strengthened her resolve. She knew they were taking a risk, but she also knew they had no other choice. They had to fight, and they had to do it now.

Later that evening, Mae made her way to Michael's apartment. They had agreed to meet to discuss their next steps, to figure out how to prepare for the meeting with the board. She knocked on the door, her heart racing, and he quickly opened it, pulling her inside.

"Mae," he greeted, his voice filled with relief. "I'm glad you're here."

She smiled, leaning up to kiss him softly. "Of course I'm here," she whispered. "We have work to do."

Michael nodded, leading her to the small kitchen table where they had spread out papers, notes, and evidence they had gathered. "We need to be ready for anything," he said, his tone serious. "The dean isn't going to back down easily, and we need to anticipate every move she might make."

Mae nodded, her eyes scanning the documents. "I've been thinking," she began slowly, "maybe we need to go beyond just defending ourselves. Maybe we need to go on the offensive."

Michael looked at her, his brow furrowing. "What do you mean?"

"I mean," Mae continued, "we need to show that this isn't just about us. We need to expose the double standards, the hypocrisy. If we can dig deeper, find more evidence of misconduct or bias within the administration, it might be enough to force their hand."

Michael considered her words carefully, his eyes thoughtful. "It's risky," he said finally. "But you're right. If we want to win, we need to be proactive. We need to show that we're not the ones who should be on trial here."

Mae felt a surge of determination. "Exactly," she agreed. "And I think I know where we can start."

Michael leaned forward, his eyes bright with interest. "Where?"

"Tom," Mae said, her voice steady. "He's been trying to undermine us from the beginning, and I think he knows more than he's letting on. If we can find out what he's hiding, we might be able to turn the tables on him — and the administration."

Michael nodded slowly, his expression serious. "It's a long shot," he said, "but it's worth a try. How do you want to approach it?"

Mae smiled, a small, determined smile. "I'll handle it," she replied. "I think I can get him to talk. I just need to find the right moment."

The next day, Mae kept an eye out for Tom, watching for an opportunity to confront him alone. She knew it wouldn't be easy — he was wary, always looking over his shoulder, and she needed to be careful not to spook him. But she was determined to find out what he knew.

Finally, she saw him heading toward the library, his expression tense, his steps quick. Mae followed him, keeping her distance, watching as he made his way to a quiet corner of the building, away from the crowds. She waited until he was alone, then approached, her heart pounding in her chest.

"Tom," she called softly, her voice calm but firm.

He turned, his eyes narrowing when he saw her. "Mae," he replied, his tone guarded. "What do you want?"

Mae took a deep breath, stepping closer. "I want to talk," she said evenly. "I want to know why you're doing this. Why you're trying so hard to destroy me and Michael."

Tom snorted, crossing his arms over his chest. "Destroy you?" he scoffed. "You've done that to yourselves. I'm just exposing the truth."

"But why?" Mae pressed, her eyes searching his. "What's in it for you, Tom? Why do you care so much about what happens to us?"

Tom hesitated, his gaze flicking away for a moment. "Maybe I don't like seeing people get away with things," he muttered. "Maybe I think you're both hypocrites."

Mae stepped even closer, her voice softening. "Or maybe," she said gently, "there's something more. Something you're not telling us."

Tom's face tightened, a flash of anger crossing his eyes. "You don't know anything," he snapped. "You're just trying to deflect, trying to make me look like the bad guy."

Mae held her ground, refusing to back down. "I'm not trying to make you look like anything," she said quietly. "I'm just trying to understand. And if there's something I need to know, something that could help us both... I think you should tell me."

Tom stared at her for a long moment, his expression hard, his eyes cold. Then, slowly, he seemed to soften, his shoulders relaxing just a bit. "You think you know so much," he muttered, his voice low. "But you don't know the half of it."

Mae felt a flicker of hope. "Then tell me," she urged. "Help me understand."

Tom hesitated again, then sighed, his gaze dropping to the floor. "Fine," he said finally. "I'll tell you. But you're not going to like it."

Mae held her breath, her heart racing. "Try me," she whispered.

Tom looked up, his eyes dark with anger and something else, something that looked like pain. "It's not just about you and Michael," he began, his voice rough. "It's about what happened to me... to someone I cared about."

Mae frowned, confused. "What do you mean?"

Tom clenched his jaw, his hands tightening into fists. "My sister," he said quietly. "She was a student here. And she got involved with a professor. Just like you. But when things went wrong, no one believed her. No one listened. They protected him, and she was the one who paid the price."

Mae felt a wave of sympathy wash over her. "I'm... I'm sorry, Tom," she whispered. "I didn't know."

Tom's eyes blazed with anger. "No, you didn't," he snapped. "And that's why I'm not going to let it happen again. Not to anyone else."

Mae swallowed hard, her heart aching. "I understand why you're angry," she said softly. "But Michael isn't like that. We're not like that."

Tom shook his head, his face hard. "Maybe not," he muttered. "But how do I know that? How does anyone know that?"

Mae stepped closer, her voice filled with sincerity. "Because we're telling the truth," she said firmly. "And we're willing to fight for it. Just like you're fighting for your sister."

Tom looked at her for a long moment, his expression conflicted, his jaw clenched. "Maybe," he said finally, his voice softer. "But if you're lying... if you're just trying to save yourselves... I swear I'll take you down."

Mae nodded, her eyes steady. "I'm not lying," she whispered. "And if you give us a chance, I think you'll see that."

Tom stared at her, his eyes searching hers, and for a moment, Mae felt like he might actually believe her, that they might actually find common ground. But then, his face hardened again, and he turned away. "We'll see," he muttered. "We'll see."

Mae watched him go, her heart pounding, her mind racing. She didn't know if she had gotten through to him, but she knew she had to try. She turned and headed back to Michael, ready to share what she had learned, ready to keep fighting.

Chapter 20: The Final Countdown

Mae felt the weight of the last few days pressing heavily on her shoulders as she made her way back to Michael's apartment. Her conversation with Tom lingered in her mind, a mix of unexpected sympathy and unresolved tension swirling within her. She had glimpsed a different side of him, a side driven by pain and a need for justice, even if it was misplaced. She couldn't help but wonder if there was a way to turn this around, to find common ground that might help their cause.

When she reached Michael's door, she knocked softly, her heart still racing from the encounter. He opened it quickly, his face lighting up with relief as he saw her. "Mae," he breathed, pulling her into a tight hug. "I've been worried. How did it go?"

She leaned into his embrace, taking a moment to steady herself, to find the right words. "It was... complicated," she admitted, pulling back to look up at him. "I talked to Tom. He's not just trying to sabotage us — he's angry because of what happened to his sister. She was involved with a professor here, and things went bad. He thinks we're just another version of the same story."

Michael's face darkened with concern. "I had no idea," he murmured. "That explains a lot... but it doesn't make things easier."

"No," Mae agreed, "but it might be an opportunity. If we can show him that we're different, that we're not hiding or running away, maybe we can at least neutralize him. Maybe we can get him to back off, or even help us."

Michael nodded slowly, his hand running through his hair. "It's worth a shot," he said finally. "But we need to be careful. If he decides to push harder, he could still cause a lot of damage."

"I know," Mae replied, her voice firm. "But I think he's open to listening. He's angry, but he's also hurting. If we can appeal to that, we might have a chance."

Michael gave her a small, encouraging smile. "You've always been good at seeing the best in people," he said softly, his hand brushing her cheek. "It's one of the things I love about you."

Mae felt a warmth spread through her chest at his words, her heart swelling with affection. "I just want to do what's right," she whispered. "For us, and for everyone else caught in the middle."

He kissed her gently, a soft, lingering kiss that made her forget the world outside, if only for a moment. "We will," he murmured against her lips. "We'll find a way."

The following days were a blur of preparation and anticipation. The protest idea quickly gained traction, and within hours, news spread like wildfire across campus. Mae, Jess, and a small group of other students worked tirelessly to organize it, crafting signs, preparing chants, and reaching out to local media to ensure they had coverage.

Mae felt a renewed sense of purpose as she worked, the energy of those around her bolstering her resolve. They had decided to hold the protest two days before the board was set to reconvene, hoping to sway public opinion and put pressure on the administration to reconsider its stance. It was a bold move, but Mae knew they needed to do something drastic if they were going to change the course of events.

On the morning of the protest, Mae arrived at the administration building early. The air was crisp and cool, a light breeze rustling the leaves overhead. She could feel the tension building, the anticipation buzzing like electricity around her. A small crowd had already gathered, and she recognized a few familiar faces — students, professors, even some local journalists with cameras slung over their shoulders.

Jess approached her, her face bright with excitement. "We're getting a good turnout," she said, her voice filled with hope. "People are listening, Mae. This might actually work."

Mae nodded, her heart racing with both fear and excitement. "I hope so," she replied. "We need to show them that we're not going to back down, that we're not afraid."

As the crowd grew, Mae spotted Michael in the distance, talking with a group of faculty members who had come to support them. He looked over and gave her a small nod, a reassuring smile that made her feel a little stronger, a little braver.

She took a deep breath, stepping up onto a small platform they had set up in front of the building. The crowd quieted, their eyes turning to her, waiting to hear what she had to say.

"Thank you all for coming," Mae began, her voice steady despite the nerves fluttering in her stomach. "We're here today because we believe in something important — the right to be heard, the right to stand up against injustice, the right to love who we choose without fear of retribution."

There were murmurs of agreement, nods from the crowd, and Mae felt a surge of confidence. "The administration wants to silence us, to make an example of us," she continued. "But we won't be silenced. We won't be intimidated. We will fight for our rights, for our future, and for each other."

The crowd cheered, a wave of support that washed over her, giving her strength. She glanced over at Michael, who was watching her with a look of pride and love that made her heart swell.

"This isn't just about Michael and me," Mae went on, her voice growing stronger. "This is about all of us — students, faculty, everyone who believes in fairness, in justice, in standing up for what's right. If we let them win, if we let them silence us, then we all lose."

More cheers erupted from the crowd, and Mae felt a flicker of hope ignite in her chest. She could see the impact her words were having, could feel the momentum building.

She continued to speak, rallying the crowd, calling for change, for action, for courage. And as she spoke, she felt the fear and doubt that had plagued her for days begin to melt away, replaced by a fierce determination to see this through to the end.

As the protest continued, Mae moved through the crowd, talking to students, answering questions from reporters, feeling a sense of solidarity and purpose that strengthened her resolve. She knew they were making a difference, that they were being heard.

But then, out of the corner of her eye, she spotted Tom standing on the fringes of the crowd, his arms crossed over his chest, his expression unreadable. Mae felt a jolt of nervousness but also a flicker of hope. Maybe this was her chance to talk to him again, to see if she could get through to him.

She made her way over, her heart pounding. "Tom," she called out as she approached, "can we talk?"

He glanced at her, his eyes wary, but he didn't walk away. "What do you want, Mae?" he asked, his tone guarded.

"I just want to know where you stand," she said softly. "You've seen what we're trying to do here, what we're fighting for. Are you still against us?"

Tom looked away, his jaw tight. "I don't know," he muttered. "I still don't trust you. But... I see what you're trying to do."

Mae took a step closer, her voice earnest. "We're not the enemy, Tom," she whispered. "We're just trying to fight for what's right. For all of us."

Tom was silent for a long moment, his expression conflicted. Then he sighed, his shoulders sagging slightly. "Maybe," he said quietly. "But I'm still watching you. I'm not convinced yet."

Mae nodded, understanding. "That's fair," she replied. "Just... keep watching. See for yourself what we're about."

Tom gave her a long, searching look, then nodded. "Alright," he said finally. "I'll see."

Mae felt a small flicker of hope. It wasn't much, but it was something. A step in the right direction. She turned back to the crowd, ready to keep fighting, knowing that every small victory mattered.

By the time the protest ended, Mae felt exhausted but exhilarated. They had made their voices heard, and she could see the impact it was having on the people around her. There was a sense of momentum, a feeling that they were finally pushing back against the administration's control.

As the crowd began to disperse, Michael came over to her, his face glowing with pride. "You were incredible," he murmured, pulling her into a tight embrace. "I'm so proud of you."

Mae smiled, resting her head against his chest. "We did this together," she whispered. "And we're not done yet."

He kissed her softly, a slow, tender kiss that made her heart skip a beat. "No," he agreed, "we're not done yet. But today... today was a good day."

Mae nodded, feeling a swell of emotion. "It was," she whispered. "And we're going to keep fighting. For us, for everyone."

Michael held her close, his arms wrapped around her, and for a moment, everything felt right. They still had a long way to go, but they had each other, and they had hope. And that was enough.

As they stood there, wrapped in each other's arms, Mae felt a sense of calm wash over her. She didn't know what the future held, but she knew they would face it together, side by side, no matter what.

Chapter 21: Shadows of Doubt

The morning after the protest, the campus was abuzz with chatter. Mae could feel a shift in the air, a mix of anticipation, fear, and something that felt almost like hope. The protest had drawn more attention than she'd expected — the local news had picked up the story, and social media was flooded with posts and videos of the rally, students holding signs, chanting for justice, for change. She could see the impact of their efforts, but she knew that the real battle was still ahead. The board meeting loomed like a storm cloud on the horizon, and they had no idea how the administration would react.

Mae sat in the dining hall, surrounded by the familiar hum of voices and clattering of trays, her mind racing with thoughts of the meeting and their next steps. She looked down at her phone, scrolling through the news articles and comments. Most of them were supportive, but there were still some filled with doubt, skepticism, and outright hostility. She couldn't help but feel a knot of anxiety forming in her stomach.

Michael slid into the seat across from her, his expression tense but determined. "Morning," he said softly, reaching out to take her hand. "How are you holding up?"

"I'm okay," Mae replied, squeezing his hand. "Just... nervous, I guess. The protest went well, but I'm worried about how the administration is going to respond. They're not going to take this lying down."

Michael nodded, his brow furrowing. "I know," he said quietly. "But we made our stand, and we have more support now than we did before. That's something."

Mae smiled weakly. "I hope it's enough," she whispered. "I hope we didn't just provoke them to come down harder."

Michael leaned in, his voice low and reassuring. "We knew this would be a fight," he murmured. "And we're ready for it. We've already come this far, and we're not turning back now."

Mae nodded, taking a deep breath. "You're right," she agreed. "We have to keep pushing, keep fighting."

As the day went on, Mae found herself moving through campus with renewed purpose. She knew they needed to stay visible, to keep the momentum going, and to make sure the administration knew they weren't going to back down. She and Jess spent hours talking to students, gathering signatures for a petition, and organizing another meeting to plan their next steps.

By the afternoon, Mae felt a mix of exhaustion and exhilaration. The response had been overwhelming — more students and faculty were stepping forward to support them, to speak out against the administration's actions. She felt a flicker of hope, a sense that maybe they were finally starting to turn the tide.

But then, just as she was beginning to feel a little more confident, she received a text message from an unknown number. Her heart skipped a beat as she opened it, her eyes scanning the screen.

Unknown: *Meet me in the basement of the library. 6 PM. It's important.*

Mae frowned, her mind racing. She didn't recognize the number, and there was no indication of who the message was from. But something about it felt urgent, almost desperate.

She hesitated for a moment, then quickly typed a reply.

Mae: *Who is this? Why do you want to meet?*

A few seconds later, another message came through.

Unknown: *You want to know what's really going on? Meet me. 6 PM. Don't bring anyone.*

Mae felt a shiver run down her spine. She glanced around, her eyes scanning the faces of the students passing by. She didn't know what to make of the message, but she had a feeling it was important.

She looked at her watch — it was already 5:30 PM. She didn't have much time to decide. Taking a deep breath, she stood up and started walking toward the library, her heart pounding with a mix of curiosity and fear.

The basement of the library was dimly lit, the flickering fluorescent lights casting eerie shadows on the walls. Mae descended the stairs slowly, her footsteps echoing in the quiet. She felt a knot of anxiety tightening in her stomach, her senses on high alert.

When she reached the bottom of the stairs, she paused, listening for any sound, any indication of who might be waiting for her. She heard nothing but the faint hum of the lights, the distant rustle of papers from somewhere deeper in the basement.

"Hello?" she called out softly, her voice trembling slightly. "I'm here. Who are you?"

There was a moment of silence, and then a figure stepped out from behind a row of shelves. Mae's eyes widened in surprise as she recognized him — it was Alex, the tech-savvy student who had helped her and Michael retrieve the emails.

"Alex," she breathed, her heart racing. "What are you doing here? Why did you text me?"

Alex glanced around nervously, his face pale and tense. "I had to talk to you," he whispered urgently. "I found something...

something big. But I can't be seen talking to you out in the open. Not right now."

Mae felt a surge of anxiety. "What did you find?" she asked, her voice low. "Is it about Dean Caldwell?"

Alex nodded quickly, stepping closer. "Yes," he said, "and more than that. I've been digging deeper into the administration's records, and I found something... something that could change everything."

Mae's pulse quickened. "What is it?" she pressed, her voice filled with urgency.

Alex glanced around again, his eyes darting nervously. "It's a financial trail," he whispered. "Payments, favors, all sorts of things. There are connections between the dean and several board members. It looks like they've been involved in some sort of cover-up, using university funds for... well, let's just say, questionable purposes."

Mae felt a shock of disbelief. "Are you serious?" she whispered. "Do you have proof?"

Alex nodded, pulling out a flash drive from his pocket. "I copied everything," he said, holding it out to her. "Emails, bank records, internal memos. If we release this, it will blow the whole thing wide open."

Mae's hand trembled as she reached for the drive. "This could be exactly what we need," she murmured, her mind racing with the implications. "But... it's dangerous, Alex. If they find out you were digging around..."

Alex shrugged, his face tense but resolute. "I know," he said quietly. "But I believe in what you and Michael are doing. This place needs to change, and if this can help, then it's worth the risk."

Mae felt a surge of gratitude and fear. "Thank you," she whispered, clutching the drive tightly. "I promise we'll use this carefully."

Alex nodded, his expression serious. "Just... be careful," he warned. "They're not going to go down without a fight."

"We will," Mae promised, feeling a mix of determination and anxiety. "We'll be ready."

Mae left the library, her mind spinning with the new information. She hurried to find Michael, her heart racing with both excitement and fear. When she finally reached his apartment, she knocked quickly, and he opened the door, his face filled with concern.

"Mae," he greeted, pulling her inside. "What's going on? You look like you've seen a ghost."

She held up the flash drive, her eyes wide. "Alex found something," she said quickly. "Something big. Financial records, emails, evidence of corruption within the administration. This could be our ticket."

Michael's eyes widened in surprise and hope. "Are you serious?" he asked, taking the drive from her. "This... this could change everything."

"I know," Mae replied, her voice trembling with emotion. "But we need to be careful. If we release this too soon, or if we don't have the right strategy, it could backfire. We need to figure out the best way to use this."

Michael nodded, his face filled with determination. "We'll go through it tonight," he said. "We'll make a plan. We have to make sure we do this right."

Mae felt a surge of relief, knowing they were in this together, ready to face whatever came next. "Yes," she agreed, "we'll do it together."

They spent the rest of the evening pouring over the documents, their heads bent together, their minds racing with possibilities. The evidence was damning — emails detailing questionable financial transactions, records of favors exchanged between the dean and several board members, all pointing to a pattern of corruption and misuse of university funds.

"This is it," Michael murmured, his voice filled with awe. "This is the leverage we need."

"But how do we use it?" Mae asked, her brow furrowed. "If we just leak it to the press, they'll try to discredit us, say we fabricated it. We need to present it in a way they can't refute."

Michael thought for a moment, his eyes narrowing. "What if we go to the board directly?" he suggested. "Before the meeting. Present the evidence to them, force their hand. If they see this, they might realize they have no choice but to back down."

Mae nodded slowly, considering the idea. "It's risky," she said, "but it might be our best shot. If we can convince them that exposing this will hurt the university more than it hurts us, they might be willing to listen."

"Exactly," Michael agreed. "We'll go to them first thing in the morning. We'll make our case, and we won't back down."

Mae felt a surge of adrenaline, her heart racing with both fear and hope. "Okay," she said, her voice firm. "Let's do it. We have nothing left to lose."

The next morning, Mae and Michael made their way to the administration building, their hearts pounding with anticipation. They had arranged a meeting with the board, under the pretext of discussing the upcoming hearing. As they entered the building, they could feel the tension in the air, the weight of what was about to happen pressing down on them.

They were escorted to a small conference room where the board members were already gathered, their expressions serious and guarded. Dean Caldwell sat at the head of the table, her eyes narrowed as she watched them enter.

"You requested a meeting," she said coldly. "What is this about?"

Michael took a deep breath, stepping forward. "We wanted to discuss the hearing tomorrow," he began, "but first, we need to address something else."

He placed the flash drive on the table, sliding it toward the dean. "This contains evidence of financial misconduct," he continued, his voice steady. "Emails, bank records, internal memos — all pointing to a pattern of corruption within this administration."

There was a murmur among the board members, a ripple of shock and uncertainty. Dean Caldwell's face paled, her hands clenching into fists on the table.

"This is absurd," she snapped. "You think you can blackmail us?"

"We're not here to blackmail anyone," Mae interjected, her voice calm but firm. "We're here to demand fairness. If you're going to accuse us of misconduct, you need to be held to the same standard. We all know that if this evidence goes public, it will cause a scandal that could destroy the university's reputation."

Dean Caldwell's eyes flashed with anger, but Mae could see the fear behind them, the realization that they were cornered.

"You have until tomorrow to decide," Michael added. "Withdraw the charges against us, or we release the evidence to the press. It's your choice."

The room fell silent, every eye on the dean. Mae held her breath, waiting, hoping that they had done enough, that they had finally turned the tables.

After what felt like an eternity, Dean Caldwell finally spoke, her voice tight with rage. "We will... consider your request," she said slowly, her eyes blazing with fury. "But don't think for a moment that this is over."

Mae nodded, her heart pounding. "We'll be waiting," she replied, her voice steady. "And we're not afraid."

She and Michael turned and walked out of the room, their heads held high, their hearts racing with adrenaline. They had taken a risk, a huge gamble, but it had paid off. They had forced the administration's hand, and now, all they could do was wait and see what would happen next.

As they stepped outside, Michael took her hand, squeezing it tightly. "We did it," he whispered, a smile spreading across his face. "We actually did it."

Mae smiled back, feeling a surge of hope and determination. "Yes," she whispered, "but it's not over yet. We still have to see this through."

Michael nodded, his eyes filled with resolve. "And we will," he promised. "Together."

Chapter 23: The Moment of Reckoning

The morning of the board meeting dawned with a thick fog rolling over the campus, a shroud of mist that seemed to mirror the uncertainty that had settled over everyone. Mae woke up with a heavy sense of anticipation weighing on her chest, her thoughts spinning like a carousel that wouldn't slow down. She and Michael had made their move, placed their cards on the table, and now all they could do was wait and see how the administration would respond.

She got dressed quickly, her hands trembling slightly as she buttoned her shirt. She glanced at her phone, half expecting — half dreading — to see a message from Michael. But there was nothing. Just the cold, empty silence of the early morning. Taking a deep breath, she grabbed her bag and headed out the door, the chill of the fog wrapping around her like a second skin.

When she reached the courtyard in front of the administration building, she saw Michael standing there, waiting for her. His face was tense, his hands shoved deep into his pockets. He looked up as she approached, a small, strained smile touching his lips.

"Mae," he greeted, his voice low. "You okay?"

"As okay as I can be," she replied, trying to muster a smile of her own. "How about you?"

He shrugged, a wry grin crossing his face. "Nervous as hell," he admitted. "But ready. We've done everything we can. Now, it's up to them."

Mae nodded, reaching for his hand. "Whatever happens," she whispered, "we face it together."

Michael squeezed her hand tightly. "Together," he agreed.

The board meeting was scheduled for 9 AM, and as the time drew closer, the tension around the administration building grew thicker. Students and faculty gathered in small groups, whispering among themselves, their faces filled with curiosity and anxiety. Mae could see a few reporters hovering at the edges of the crowd, their cameras ready, their eyes scanning for any sign of drama.

Jess joined them a few minutes later, her expression grim. "They're going to try to drag this out," she said quietly. "Make it seem like they're taking it seriously, but really just trying to buy time."

"We expected that," Michael replied, his voice calm. "But they can't ignore the evidence. Not forever."

"No," Jess agreed, "but they'll do whatever they can to protect themselves. Be ready for anything."

Mae felt a flicker of unease at Jess's words but pushed it aside. They were here, and they were ready. There was no turning back now.

At exactly 9 AM, the doors to the administration building opened, and a staff member stepped out, beckoning Mae and Michael forward. "The board is ready to see you," she announced, her voice clipped and formal.

Mae took a deep breath, her heart pounding in her chest. She glanced at Michael, who gave her a small nod, and together, they walked up the steps and into the building, the doors closing behind them with a heavy thud.

The conference room was cold and impersonal, the long table surrounded by somber-faced board members. Dean Caldwell sat at the head, her expression as frosty as ever, her hands folded neatly in front of her. Mae and Michael took their seats at the end of the table, their backs straight, their eyes steady.

"Thank you for coming," Dean Caldwell began, her tone icy. "We have reviewed the materials you provided, and we are prepared to discuss our findings."

Michael nodded, his face calm. "We're here to listen," he replied. "And to ensure that this process is fair."

The dean's eyes narrowed slightly. "We will see," she said. "Now, before we proceed, I must remind you that this is a formal hearing. Anything you say can and will be recorded for our records."

"Understood," Mae replied, her voice steady. "We're ready."

Dean Caldwell nodded curtly, then turned to the board members. "We have reviewed the evidence provided by Mr. Arden and Ms. Larson," she continued, "and while there are certainly concerning elements, we must also consider the source and the manner in which this information was obtained."

Mae felt a flicker of anger at the insinuation but kept her expression neutral. They had expected this — the attempt to discredit them, to make it seem like they were the ones in the wrong.

"However," the dean went on, her voice cold, "we cannot ignore the implications of what we have seen. Therefore, we have decided to conduct a full internal investigation into these matters. In the meantime, we are placing Mr. Arden on temporary administrative leave."

Mae's heart sank, a wave of fear crashing over her. "Administrative leave?" she echoed, her voice tight with emotion. "But that's—"

"A precaution," Dean Caldwell interrupted sharply. "While we determine the validity of these claims and assess any potential damage to the university's reputation."

Michael's face remained calm, but Mae could see the tension in his jaw, the way his hands gripped the edge of the table. "I understand the need for an investigation," he said carefully, "but placing me on leave seems... excessive, given the circumstances."

"It is a necessary step," the dean replied, her eyes cold. "To ensure that there is no further disruption to the campus environment."

Mae felt a surge of frustration. "And what about the evidence?" she demanded. "The emails, the financial records — are you just going to sweep that under the rug?"

Dean Caldwell's face tightened, a flicker of irritation crossing her eyes. "We will address those matters in due course," she said coolly. "But for now, our primary concern is maintaining order and protecting the integrity of this institution."

Mae's hands clenched into fists under the table. She could feel the anger bubbling inside her, the sense of injustice burning in her chest. But she forced herself to stay calm, to breathe, to think.

"And what about Mae?" Michael asked, his voice steady. "Is she to be punished as well, for daring to speak out?"

Dean Caldwell hesitated for a moment, then shook her head. "Ms. Larson will not face any disciplinary action at this time," she said. "However, we strongly advise her to refrain from any further... disruptions."

Mae felt a surge of relief mixed with frustration. They were trying to placate her, to keep her quiet. But she wasn't about to be silenced.

"We will comply with the investigation," Michael said firmly, "but we expect it to be fair and transparent. We have nothing to hide."

Dean Caldwell's eyes flicked to him, a small, cold smile playing at her lips. "I'm sure you believe that, Mr. Arden," she replied. "But we shall see."

Mae felt a chill run down her spine. She could sense the underlying threat in the dean's words, the promise of a fight that was far from over.

"Thank you for your time," Michael said, standing up. "We look forward to your findings."

Mae stood as well, her heart pounding in her chest. She could feel the eyes of the board members on her, could sense their doubt, their suspicion. But she refused to be intimidated. She held her head high, her gaze steady.

As they turned to leave, Dean Caldwell's voice stopped them. "One more thing," she said, her tone deceptively casual. "We will be closely monitoring all activities related to this case. Any further attempts to undermine this investigation will not be tolerated."

Mae turned back, meeting the dean's gaze head-on. "We have no intention of undermining anything," she replied evenly. "We just want the truth."

Dean Caldwell's smile was thin, almost predatory. "As do we," she said. "Good day, Ms. Larson. Mr. Arden."

They walked out of the room, their steps measured, their hearts racing. As soon as they were outside, Mae let out a breath she hadn't realized she'd been holding.

"Well," Michael said quietly, "that went about as expected."

"They're playing for time," Mae murmured, her voice filled with frustration. "They're trying to stall, to make it seem like they're doing something while they figure out how to cover their tracks."

Michael nodded, his expression serious. "But they know we're not backing down," he said. "And they know we have the evidence. They're scared, Mae. We just have to keep the pressure on."

Mae felt a surge of determination. "Then that's exactly what we'll do," she agreed. "We'll keep pushing until they have no choice but to face the truth."

Michael smiled, a small, fierce smile. "That's my girl," he said softly, pulling her into a tight embrace. "We're in this together. And we're going to win."

Mae hugged him back, feeling the strength in his arms, the steady beat of his heart. "Yes," she whispered, "together."

The rest of the day passed in a blur of activity. Mae and Michael spent hours meeting with their supporters, planning their next moves, strategizing how to keep the pressure on the administration. They knew they had to stay visible, to keep the momentum going, to make it impossible for the administration to sweep this under the rug.

As the afternoon wore on, Mae found herself back in the student union, surrounded by a small group of students who were eager to help. They were discussing their next steps when she felt a tap on her shoulder.

She turned to see Tom standing there, his face tense, his eyes filled with uncertainty. "Mae," he said quietly, "can we talk?"

Mae hesitated for a moment, then nodded. "Of course," she replied, stepping away from the group. "What's on your mind?"

Tom glanced around, making sure no one was listening. "I've been thinking," he began slowly. "About what you said... about your fight for fairness."

Mae nodded, her heart racing. "And?" she prompted gently.

"And I've been watching," he continued, his voice low. "I still don't trust you completely, but... I think you're telling the truth. I think you really believe in what you're doing."

Mae felt a flicker of hope. "I do," she said firmly. "And I want to make this right, for everyone."

Tom sighed, rubbing the back of his neck. "I still have my doubts," he admitted, "but... I'm willing to help. If there's a way I can make sure this is handled fairly, I'll do it."

Mae's eyes widened in surprise. "You'd help us?" she asked cautiously.

Tom nodded, his expression serious. "I can't promise much," he said, "but I have some contacts... people who might be able to shed light on what's really going on. If I find anything, I'll let you know."

Mae smiled, a genuine smile of gratitude. "Thank you, Tom," she said softly. "That means a lot."

He nodded, his face still guarded but less hostile. "Just... don't make me regret it," he muttered, before turning and walking away.

Mae watched him go, a small spark of hope igniting in her chest. She turned back to the group, her resolve renewed.

"We keep pushing," she said firmly. "We keep fighting. We're not done yet."

The group nodded in agreement, their faces filled with determination. Mae knew they had a long road ahead, but for the first time, she felt like they had a real chance. They were in this together, and they were going to see it through to the end.

And as the day wore on, Mae felt a quiet strength settle over her, a sense of purpose that steadied her nerves and calmed her fears.

Chapter 24: The Fallout Begins

The hours after the board meeting seemed to stretch on endlessly, every minute feeling like an eternity as Mae and Michael waited for news, for any sign of what the administration might do next. The campus buzzed with speculation, students and faculty whispering in hushed tones, their eyes following Mae and Michael whenever they passed by. Mae could feel the weight of their scrutiny, their curiosity, their doubt, but she refused to let it show. She had to stay strong, for Michael, for herself, for everyone who was counting on them.

They met in the student union later that afternoon, sitting at a corner table with Jess and a few other supporters. Michael's expression was tense, his fingers drumming nervously on the table as he listened to Jess's report.

"There's definitely a lot of talk," Jess was saying, her voice low but urgent. "People are paying attention. But it's hard to tell which way it's going to go. Some of the faculty are getting nervous — they don't want to be caught in the middle of a scandal."

"That's exactly what the administration wants," Michael muttered, his jaw tight. "They want to scare people into silence, make it look like we're the problem, not them."

Mae nodded, her brow furrowed in thought. "We need to keep the pressure on," she said. "We can't let them control the narrative. We have to make sure people see what's really happening."

Jess sighed, rubbing her temples. "Easier said than done," she replied. "They've got years of experience spinning things their way. And they've got resources — lawyers, PR people, money."

"We have the truth," Mae countered, her voice firm. "And we have people who believe in us, who are willing to stand up with us. That's got to count for something."

Michael reached over, squeezing her hand. "It does," he agreed softly. "But we need to be smart about this. We can't afford any mistakes."

Mae nodded, feeling a surge of determination. "No mistakes," she echoed. "We do this right, or we don't do it at all."

As the day wore on, Mae continued to reach out to supporters, organizing meetings, gathering signatures for petitions, doing everything she could to keep the momentum going. She knew they were fighting an uphill battle, but she refused to give up. She had promised Michael that they would see this through together, and she intended to keep that promise.

By late afternoon, she was back in the student union, sitting with a small group of students who were working on a statement for the campus newspaper. She felt a mix of exhaustion and adrenaline, her mind racing with plans, ideas, strategies.

Suddenly, her phone buzzed in her pocket. She pulled it out, glancing at the screen. It was a text from an unknown number.

Unknown: *Meet me at the old science building. Now. Come alone.*

Mae frowned, her heart skipping a beat. She hesitated for a moment, then quickly typed a reply.

Mae: *Who is this?*

Almost immediately, another message came through.

Unknown: *It's important. Trust me.*

Mae felt a shiver run down her spine. She glanced around, her mind racing with possibilities. She knew it could be a trap, another attempt by the administration to intimidate her. But something told her she needed to go, to find out who was reaching out and why.

She stood up, slipping her phone into her pocket. "I need to go," she said to the group. "I'll be back soon."

"Where are you going?" one of the students asked, a note of concern in her voice.

"Just... meeting someone," Mae replied, trying to keep her tone casual. "I'll explain later."

The student nodded, but Mae could see the worry in her eyes. She turned and walked quickly out of the building, her heart pounding as she made her way across campus toward the old science building.

The old science building was one of the oldest structures on campus, a dark, looming silhouette against the fading light. Mae approached cautiously, her footsteps echoing on the cracked pavement. She glanced around, her senses on high alert, her breath coming in short, nervous bursts.

When she reached the door, she hesitated, her hand hovering over the handle. She took a deep breath, steeling herself, then pushed the door open and stepped inside.

The interior was dimly lit, the faint glow of emergency lights casting long shadows on the walls. Mae moved slowly, her ears straining for any sound, any sign of who might be waiting for her.

"Mae," a voice called softly from the shadows. "Over here."

She turned, her heart skipping a beat as she saw a figure emerge from the darkness. It was Tom. He looked nervous, his hands shoved deep into his pockets, his eyes darting around as if he expected someone to jump out at any moment.

"Tom," Mae breathed, a mix of relief and confusion flooding her senses. "What are you doing here?"

He stepped closer, his face tense. "I needed to talk to you," he whispered urgently. "I think I've found something... something you need to see."

Mae felt a surge of anxiety. "What is it?" she asked, her voice low.

Tom glanced around again, his eyes filled with fear. "I've been digging," he admitted. "I wanted to find out what's really going on, to make sure you weren't just playing me. And I found something... something big."

Mae's pulse quickened. "What did you find?" she pressed.

Tom hesitated, then pulled out his phone, holding it up for her to see. "I found emails," he said quietly. "Between the dean and a few key board members. They're planning something, Mae. Something to shut you down for good."

Mae felt a chill run down her spine. "What do you mean?" she whispered, her eyes scanning the screen. "What are they planning?"

Tom glanced around nervously again. "They're going to push forward with the investigation, but they're going to frame it as a way to protect the university," he explained. "They're going to make it look like you and Michael are the ones causing all the trouble, like you're the ones trying to tear the place apart."

Mae's heart pounded in her chest. "But that's not true," she protested. "We're fighting for fairness, for the truth!"

Tom nodded, his face grim. "I know," he said. "But they're going to spin it, make it look like you're radicals, like you're trying to bring the university down. They're already working with a PR firm, getting ready to launch a full-blown smear campaign."

Mae felt a wave of anger and fear crash over her. "How do you know all this?" she asked.

Tom sighed, rubbing the back of his neck. "I still have some contacts," he said quietly. "People who know things, people who owe me favors. They sent me these emails. They wanted me to know what I was getting into."

Mae stared at him, her mind racing. "Why are you telling me this?" she asked finally. "I thought you didn't trust me."

Tom shrugged, his face conflicted. "Maybe I still don't," he admitted. "But I don't trust them either. And I think... I think you might actually be on the right side of this."

Mae felt a flicker of hope. "Thank you," she said softly. "This means a lot."

Tom nodded, his expression serious. "Just be careful," he warned. "They're not going to play fair. And they're not going to give up."

"Neither are we," Mae replied firmly. "We're in this for the long haul."

Tom gave her a small, reluctant smile. "Good," he said quietly. "Because you're going to need all the help you can get."

Mae nodded, feeling a surge of determination. "Then let's get to work," she said. "We've got a fight on our hands."

Mae hurried back to Michael's apartment, her mind racing with everything Tom had told her. She knew they needed to act fast, to get ahead of the administration's plans. When she reached his door, she knocked quickly, and he opened it almost immediately, his face filled with concern.

"Mae," he greeted, pulling her inside. "What happened? You look like you've seen a ghost."

She quickly relayed everything Tom had told her, watching as Michael's expression shifted from concern to anger to *determination. "They're really going to try to paint us as the villains," he muttered, his jaw tight. "We can't let them do that."*

"No," Mae agreed, "but we need to be smart about this. If we react too quickly, it could play right into their hands."

Michael nodded, his brow furrowed in thought. "We need to get ahead of their narrative," he said slowly. "Show the campus — and the public — who they really are, what they're trying to do."

"We need to get those emails out," Mae added. "And we need to do it in a way that exposes their strategy without making it look like we're just trying to save ourselves."

Michael sighed, running a hand through his hair. "We need allies," he said. "People who are respected, who can vouch for us. Faculty, alumni, even members of the community. If we can build a coalition, we can make it harder for them to discredit us."

Mae nodded, her mind racing with possibilities. "We need to be strategic," she agreed. "We need to play this just right."

They spent the rest of the evening crafting a plan, reaching out to contacts, gathering support. They knew the administration would strike back, but they were ready. They were building a wall of allies, people who believed in their fight and who would stand by them when the time came.

As they worked, Mae felt a sense of calm settle over her, a quiet determination that steadied her nerves. She glanced at Michael, who was focused on the computer screen, his eyes sharp, his face set in a mask of concentration.

"We're going to win this," she whispered, almost to herself.

Michael looked up, his eyes meeting hers. "Yes," he said softly, "we are."

Chapter 25: A War of Words

The next morning, the tension on campus was palpable. Mae could feel it in the air as she made her way to the library, her steps quick and purposeful. She could see students huddled in groups, whispering with wide eyes, their expressions a mix of confusion, concern, and intrigue. She knew the administration's smear campaign had begun. The question was how far they were willing to go to discredit her and Michael — and how quickly they could counter it.

When Mae reached the library, she found Michael already there, sitting at a table with Jess and a few other supporters. His face was grim, his hands resting on a stack of papers spread out before him. He looked up as she approached, his expression softening slightly.

"Mae," he greeted, his voice low. "You saw the news?"

Mae nodded, her heart sinking. "Yeah," she replied, pulling out a chair and sitting down. "It's all over social media, too. They're accusing us of inciting unrest, of trying to undermine the administration."

Jess sighed, running a hand through her hair. "They're calling you both radicals," she said, frustration evident in her voice. "Trying to make it sound like you're out to destroy the university."

"That's exactly what Tom warned us about," Mae muttered, her jaw tight. "They're trying to frame us as the problem, to shift the focus away from their own misconduct."

Michael nodded, his face set in a hard line. "We need to act fast," he said. "We need to get ahead of their narrative, and we need to do it now."

Mae glanced around the table, seeing the worry on the faces of those around her. "We have the emails," she reminded them. "We have proof of their corruption, their attempts to manipulate this investigation. But we need to be strategic about how we release it."

Jess leaned forward, her voice urgent. "We should get it to a trusted journalist," she suggested. "Someone who can write an in-depth piece, who can expose what's really going on. If we just release the emails ourselves, they'll say we fabricated them."

Mae nodded thoughtfully. "That's a good idea," she agreed. "But we need to find someone fast. And we need to make sure they understand the full context — not just the emails, but the whole story."

Michael turned to Jess. "Do you have any contacts in the media?" he asked. "Anyone you trust?"

Jess thought for a moment, then nodded slowly. "I know a reporter at the local paper," she said. "She's been critical of the administration in the past, and she's fair. I think she'd be willing to listen."

"Great," Michael said, a flicker of hope in his eyes. "Reach out to her, see if she's interested. We need to move fast, before the administration's narrative gains too much traction."

Mae felt a surge of determination. "We should also hold another protest," she suggested. "Something big, something that shows we're not backing down. We need to keep the pressure on."

Jess nodded in agreement. "I can help organize it," she said. "We'll get the word out, make sure we have a good turnout."

"And we need to make a statement," Mae added. "Something clear and strong, outlining our position and refuting the administration's claims. We can't let them control the narrative."

Michael smiled, a small, encouraging smile. "You're right," he said softly. "We've got to fight back, on all fronts."

By midday, they were back in action, coordinating with students, faculty, and local activists. Jess reached out to her contact at the local newspaper, who agreed to meet later that afternoon to review the emails and hear their side of the story. Mae and Michael drafted a statement for the campus newspaper and began planning the next protest, setting the date for two days from now.

Mae could feel the adrenaline coursing through her veins as she moved from one task to another, her mind racing with plans and strategies. She knew they were in a precarious position, but she also knew they had the truth on their side. If they could just get it out there, if they could just make people see...

But as the afternoon wore on, Mae received another message, this time from an unknown email address. She hesitated for a moment, then opened it, her eyes scanning the screen.

Unknown: *You think you're clever, don't you? You think you can expose us and get away with it? You have no idea what you're up against. This is your last warning. Back off, or there will be consequences.*

Mae felt a chill run down her spine. She glanced around, feeling a surge of paranoia, as if she were being watched. She quickly forwarded the message to Michael, her fingers trembling slightly.

He read it, his face darkening with concern. "They're getting desperate," he murmured. "They're trying to scare us."

"It's working," Mae admitted softly. "But we can't back down now. Not when we're so close."

Michael nodded, his expression serious. "We won't," he said firmly. "But we need to be careful. We don't know how far they're willing to go."

Mae took a deep breath, steadying herself. "We've come too far to give up now," she whispered. "We have to keep fighting."

"Agreed," Michael replied, his eyes meeting hers. "But we need to stay smart. No risks we don't have to take."

Mae nodded, feeling a surge of determination. "We'll be smart," she promised. "But we won't be silenced."

Later that afternoon, Jess returned with good news. Her contact at the local newspaper, a reporter named Clara, had agreed to meet with them. Mae and Michael quickly gathered the evidence — the emails, the bank records, the internal memos — and prepared to head to the meeting.

When they arrived at the small coffee shop where Clara had agreed to meet, Mae felt a mix of nerves and excitement. She knew this was a crucial moment — if Clara believed them, if she agreed to write a story, it could change everything.

Clara was already there, sitting at a corner table with a notebook and a tape recorder in front of her. She looked up as they approached, her expression curious but guarded.

"Mae, Michael," she greeted, extending a hand. "I've heard a lot about you two these past few days."

"All good, I hope," Michael replied with a wry smile as he shook her hand.

Clara chuckled. "Depends on who you ask," she said. "But I'm here to hear your side. Let's get started."

Mae and Michael sat down, their hearts pounding as they began to lay out their case. They showed Clara the emails, explained the connections, described the administration's attempts to smear them and cover up their own misconduct.

Clara listened intently, taking notes, asking questions. Mae could see the interest growing in her eyes, the way she leaned forward, her brow furrowing in concentration.

"This is a lot," Clara said finally, glancing up from her notes. "If this is true, it's going to cause a major scandal."

"It is true," Mae insisted, her voice steady. "And it's not just about us. It's about how this administration operates, how they silence dissent, how they protect themselves at the expense of the truth."

Clara nodded slowly. "I'll need to verify everything," she said, "but if it checks out... I think there's a story here."

Michael leaned forward. "We just want a fair hearing," he said. "We want people to see what's really happening."

Clara smiled, a small, knowing smile. "I get it," she replied. "And I'll do my best to make sure they do."

Mae felt a surge of hope, a sense of relief washing over her. "Thank you," she whispered. "This means a lot."

Clara nodded, her expression serious. "Don't thank me yet," she said. "There's a lot of work to do, and this is going to make some powerful people very unhappy."

"We know," Michael replied quietly. "But we're ready for whatever comes next."

Clara gave them a long, searching look, then nodded. "I'll be in touch," she said, standing up. "Stay safe. And don't let them scare you."

Mae and Michael watched her leave, their hearts racing with a mix of fear and hope. They had taken another step, a big step, and now they just had to wait and see how it played out.

As they walked back to campus, Mae felt a sense of determination settle over her. They were fighting a war of words, a battle for truth, and they couldn't afford to lose. She knew the administration would continue to push back, to try to discredit them, but she also knew they were not alone. They had allies, they had evidence, and they had each other.

"We need to keep moving," Michael said, his voice firm. "We need to prepare for the protest, make sure it's big, make sure it sends a message."

"We will," Mae agreed. "And we need to get more faculty on our side, more people who are willing to speak out."

Michael nodded, his expression thoughtful. "I'll start reaching out tonight," he said. "We need to make sure everyone knows what's at stake."

Mae felt a surge of resolve. "We're going to win this," she whispered, almost to herself.

Michael smiled, a small, confident smile. "Yes," he said softly, "we are."

That night, Mae and Michael worked late into the evening, drafting statements, reaching out to contacts, preparing for the days ahead. They knew the administration would not back down easily, but they were ready. They had fought too hard, come too far, to give up now.

As they sat together in Michael's apartment, the glow of the computer screen lighting their faces, Mae felt a sense of calm wash over her. She didn't know what the future held, but she knew they would face it together, side by side.

"We're not done yet," she whispered, her hand resting on Michael's arm.

He turned to her, his eyes filled with determination. "No," he agreed, "not by a long shot."

Mae smiled, feeling a flicker of hope. "Then let's keep fighting," she said softly. "Let's show them who we really are."

Michael nodded, a fierce look in his eyes. "Together," he whispered.

Chapter 27: The Storm Breaks

The cheers from the crowd echoed through the courtyard, defiant and unwavering. Mae felt the adrenaline coursing through her veins, the strength of their collective voice resonating in the air around her. The police line continued to advance slowly, their faces expressionless behind dark visors, their stance a clear display of authority and intimidation. She knew the tension was reaching a breaking point. Every instinct told her that this was the moment that could make or break their movement.

Mae turned to Michael, squeezing his hand tighter. "Stay with me," she whispered, her voice barely audible over the crowd.

"Always," he replied, his eyes locked on hers, filled with determination and resolve.

She took a deep breath, stepping forward to address the crowd again. "Remember why we're here!" she shouted, her voice strong and clear. "We're here for justice, for truth, for our rights. We stand together, we stand strong, and we stand peaceful!"

The crowd responded with a roar of agreement, their voices rising in a unified chant: "Peaceful! Peaceful! Peaceful!" Mae felt a swell of pride and gratitude for their courage, for their refusal to be cowed by fear.

But as the chant grew louder, the police officers began to close in, their expressions set in stern lines. Mae could see their hands tightening on their batons, the way their shoulders tensed as if ready for a confrontation. Her heart pounded in her chest, every beat echoing like a drum in her ears.

She knew she had to act fast. She raised her hands high, palms out, in a gesture of peace. "We're here to be heard, not to fight!"

she called out. "We have a right to protest, to speak out. We are peaceful, and we will not be provoked!"

For a moment, there was a stillness, a pause that seemed to stretch on forever. Then, from somewhere in the back of the crowd, a small group of students began to kneel, raising their hands in silent protest. The gesture spread quickly, like a wave rippling through the sea of people. One by one, students and faculty alike began to kneel, raising their hands in a show of solidarity and defiance.

Mae felt tears prick at the corners of her eyes as she watched the scene unfold. They were sending a message, one that could not be ignored. She glanced at Michael, who gave her a small nod, his expression filled with pride.

"This is our moment," he murmured softly, his voice almost lost in the swell of the crowd.

Mae nodded, feeling the weight of his words. "Yes," she whispered back, "it is."

But then, a sudden commotion broke out near the edge of the courtyard. Mae turned, her heart skipping a beat as she saw a group of police officers moving quickly toward a small cluster of students who were holding signs. The officers seemed to be arguing with them, their gestures aggressive, their voices raised above the noise.

Mae felt a surge of panic. "Stay calm!" she shouted, trying to project her voice over the crowd. "Stay peaceful! Do not engage!"

But the situation was spiraling quickly. One of the officers shoved a student back, and in response, another student tried to push forward, shouting something Mae couldn't hear. The officer's hand went to his belt, and a moment later, there was a sharp, metallic sound as he drew his baton.

Mae's heart dropped into her stomach. "No!" she cried out, her voice breaking. "Please, no violence!"

The officer raised his baton, and for a split second, Mae felt time freeze. She could see the fear in the eyes of the students, the tension in the officer's stance, the ripple of uncertainty spreading through the crowd. And then, with a swift, brutal motion, the baton came down.

There was a collective gasp, a moment of shocked silence, and then chaos erupted. A scream tore through the air, followed by shouts of panic and confusion. The crowd surged backward, students pushing and shoving as they tried to move away from the officers. Mae felt herself being jostled, nearly losing her balance as the wave of people swept her to the side.

"Michael!" she shouted, reaching out for him, her heart racing with fear. "Michael!"

He grabbed her arm, pulling her close. "I'm here!" he shouted back. "We have to keep everyone calm!"

Mae nodded, swallowing her fear. She turned back to the crowd, raising her voice as loud as she could. "Everyone, please! Stay calm! Stay peaceful!"

But the panic was spreading. More officers were moving in now, their batons raised, their expressions grim. Mae could see the fear in the eyes of the students, could feel the tension rising to a breaking point.

And then, suddenly, from the back of the crowd, a voice rang out: "Let them speak! Let them protest!"

Mae turned, her breath catching in her throat as she saw Tom stepping forward, his face set in determination. "They have a right to be here!" he shouted, his voice carrying over the noise. "This is their campus too!"

For a moment, there was a stunned silence. Mae watched as Tom moved closer, his hands raised, his eyes locked on the officers. "Stand down!" he shouted. "We're not here to fight! We're here to be heard!"

The officers hesitated, their eyes flicking to one another, uncertain. Mae felt a surge of hope. Maybe, just maybe, they could still turn this around.

"He's right," Mae added quickly, her voice strong. "We have a right to be here, to protest peacefully. Please, don't escalate this."

There was a tense pause, a moment where everything seemed to hang in the balance. And then, slowly, one of the officers lowered his baton, his shoulders relaxing slightly. A murmur spread through the police line, and one by one, the officers began to lower their weapons, stepping back just a little.

Mae let out a breath she hadn't realized she was holding, relief flooding through her. She turned to Tom, her eyes wide with gratitude. "Thank you," she whispered.

Tom gave a small nod, his expression still tense but calmer. "I'm not here for you," he muttered, though his tone was softer. "I'm here for what's right."

Mae smiled, a small, tired smile. "I know," she replied, "and I'm grateful."

Michael squeezed her hand, his expression filled with pride and relief. "We did it," he murmured. "We stood our ground."

"We're not done yet," Mae replied, her voice still strong. "But we showed them we won't be silenced."

The crowd began to settle, the tension easing as the officers slowly retreated. Mae could feel the energy shifting, the fear giving way to a quiet, determined strength. They had faced down the administration's tactics, and they had not backed down.

She looked out over the sea of faces, feeling a deep sense of pride and solidarity. They had come together in the face of intimidation, in the face of fear, and they had held their ground.

"This is just the beginning," Mae called out, her voice filled with resolve. "We will continue to stand up, to speak out, to demand justice. We will not be silenced!"

Chapter 28: After the Storm

T he day after the protest, the campus felt like a different place. The air was charged with a new energy, a sense of possibility and change. Mae walked through the quad, her head held high, her steps purposeful. She could see the effect the protest had left on the students and faculty around her — a mixture of pride, solidarity, and cautious optimism. People who had previously kept their distance were now nodding to her, some even stopping to offer words of encouragement.

She had woken up to a flood of messages — texts, emails, and social media notifications — from supporters both on and off campus. The news of their protest and their stand against the administration's intimidation tactics had spread like wildfire. Local media outlets were covering the story extensively, and even some national outlets had begun to take notice. Mae felt a surge of pride and hope, knowing that they had captured the attention they needed.

But she also knew they weren't out of the woods yet. The administration wasn't going to give up easily, and they would likely try to retaliate in some way. Mae had to stay vigilant, to keep the momentum going, to ensure that their message wasn't drowned out by whatever counter-moves the administration decided to make.

As she approached the student union, she saw Michael waiting for her outside. He looked tired but energized, his eyes bright with determination. When he saw her, a smile spread across his face.

"Hey," he greeted, pulling her into a tight embrace. "You okay?"

"I'm okay," Mae replied, resting her head against his chest. "Just trying to wrap my head around everything that's happened."

Michael chuckled softly. "I know what you mean," he said. "Yesterday was... intense. But we did it, Mae. We stood our ground, and we got through to people."

Mae pulled back slightly, looking up at him. "Yeah," she agreed, "but I'm worried about what the administration will do next. They're not just going to let this go."

Michael nodded, his expression serious. "I've been thinking about that," he said. "We need to keep the pressure on. We can't let them regroup or come up with a new plan to undermine us."

"Agreed," Mae said. "And we need to reach out to more people — faculty, alumni, even donors. We need to build a coalition that's too strong for them to ignore."

Michael smiled. "I knew I loved you for a reason," he joked. "You're always two steps ahead."

Mae laughed, feeling some of the tension ease from her shoulders. "I'm just trying to think like them," she replied. "If they're going to try to cut us off, we need to show them that we're not just students with signs — we're a force they have to reckon with."

They spent the rest of the morning meeting with other student leaders and organizing committees. There was a palpable sense of unity among them now, a determination that hadn't been there before. They discussed plans for another protest, this time with even more faculty involvement, and began drafting letters to alumni and local community leaders, calling for their support.

By midday, they had gathered in a conference room in the student union to go over the next steps. Jess was there, along with several faculty members who had joined their cause. There was a mix of excitement and seriousness in the room, a sense that they were on the brink of something big.

"We need to make sure our story is front and center," Jess said, leaning over the table, her hands spread out on a stack of papers. "We've got the momentum now, but we need to keep it going. I've already reached out to a few more journalists, and they're interested in following up."

"Good," Mae replied, nodding. "But we also need to be prepared for whatever the administration throws at us next. They're not going to sit back and let us control the narrative."

One of the professors, a middle-aged woman with a kind face, leaned forward. "I've spoken to some of my colleagues," she said. "There are more faculty members who want to speak out but are afraid of losing their jobs. If we can create a safe space for them, some kind of collective statement or petition, we might be able to bring more of them on board."

Michael nodded thoughtfully. "That's a good idea," he said. "If we can show that we have faculty support, it will make it harder for the administration to dismiss us as just a bunch of unruly students."

"We could organize a town hall meeting," Mae suggested, her mind racing with possibilities. "A public forum where faculty, students, and even community members can come together and discuss these issues openly. We invite the media, make it a big event."

There were nods of agreement around the table, and Mae felt a surge of confidence. They were building something, piece by piece, moment by moment. And they weren't doing it alone.

Later that afternoon, Mae and Michael took a break to walk around the campus, their hands intertwined. The sun was shining brightly, casting long shadows across the lawn, and Mae could feel the warmth on her skin, a welcome change from the tension of the past few days.

"You know," Michael began, his tone light, "I never imagined this is where we'd end up when we started... you know, everything."

Mae smiled, squeezing his hand. "Yeah," she agreed. "I thought I'd just be navigating college life, not leading a protest against corruption and intimidation."

Michael chuckled. "You're doing an amazing job," he said softly. "I'm so proud of you."

Mae felt a flush of warmth at his words. "I'm proud of us," she replied. "We're in this together, remember?"

"Always," Michael murmured, leaning down to kiss her forehead.

They walked in comfortable silence for a while, enjoying the peace of the moment. But Mae knew it wouldn't last forever. They still had a fight ahead of them, and they needed to stay vigilant.

"What do you think the administration will do next?" she asked, breaking the quiet.

Michael sighed, his expression thoughtful. "I'm not sure," he admitted. "But I think they'll try to divide us. They'll look for weaknesses, try to find a way to undermine our support."

"We need to stay united," Mae said firmly. "We need to make sure everyone knows what's at stake."

Michael nodded. "Agreed," he said. "We'll keep building our coalition, keep reaching out to more people. And we'll be ready for whatever they throw at us."

By evening, Mae and Michael were back in the student union, finalizing their plans for the town hall meeting. They were exhausted but energized, their minds buzzing with ideas and strategies. They knew the administration would be watching closely, waiting for any opportunity to strike back, but they were ready.

Suddenly, Mae's phone buzzed with a new message. She glanced at the screen and saw it was from an unknown number. She hesitated for a moment, then opened the message.

Unknown: *Mae, it's Tom. We need to talk. Meet me in the library, third floor, now. It's important.*

Mae felt a flicker of anxiety. She turned to Michael, showing him the message. "It's from Tom," she said. "He wants to meet. Says it's important."

Michael frowned. "Do you think he's in trouble?" he asked.

"I don't know," Mae replied, feeling a knot of worry in her stomach. "But I think I should go."

Michael nodded. "Okay," he said, his voice serious. "Be careful. And call me if you need anything."

"I will," Mae promised, giving him a quick kiss before heading out the door.

When Mae reached the third floor of the library, she found Tom waiting near the back, his face tense and pale. He looked up as she approached, and Mae could see the worry in his eyes.

"Tom," she greeted cautiously. "What's going on?"

Tom glanced around, making sure they were alone. "I've been thinking," he began quietly, "about what happened yesterday, about everything that's been going on."

Mae nodded, her heart pounding. "And?" she prompted.

"I have a friend," Tom continued, his voice low. "Someone who works in the administration, who's been feeding me some information. And... I think they're planning something big. Something to really try to shut this down for good."

Mae felt a chill run down her spine. "What do you mean?" she whispered. "What are they planning?"

Tom hesitated, then took a deep breath. "They're going to threaten legal action," he said. "They're going to claim you and Michael are inciting violence, disrupting the university's operations. They're going to try to get a court order to stop all protests, to silence you."

Mae's heart sank. "But that's not true," she protested. "We've been peaceful from the start!"

Tom nodded. "I know," he said. "But they're desperate. They're going to use whatever they can to shut this down. You need to be ready."

Mae took a deep breath, trying to steady herself. "Thank you for telling me," she said softly. "We'll figure something out."

Tom nodded, his face serious. "I'm with you now," he said quietly. "I believe in what you're doing. Just... be careful, okay?"

Mae smiled, a small, grateful smile. "We will," she promised. "And thank you, Tom. This means a lot."

Tom gave a small nod, then turned and walked away, leaving Mae standing alone in the dimly lit library. She felt a mix of fear and determination rising within her. The administration was pushing back harder than ever, but they wouldn't back down. They couldn't.

Mae took a deep breath, her mind racing with possibilities. They would need to act fast, to rally their supporters, to prepare for whatever came next. She pulled out her phone and quickly typed a message to Michael.

Mae: *Just met with Tom. The administration is planning to take legal action to shut us down. We need to get ahead of this. Meet me back at the student union ASAP.*

Chapter 29: The Threat of Silence

The news of the administration's planned legal action spread quickly. By the time Mae returned to the student union, the tension in the air was almost palpable. She found Michael already there, his face serious as he spoke with Jess and a few other student leaders. When he saw Mae, he broke off mid-sentence, his expression immediately sharpening with concern.

"What did Tom say?" he asked as she approached, his voice low but urgent.

"They're planning to file for a court order," Mae replied, her tone steady but strained. "They want to accuse us of inciting violence and disrupting university operations — they're trying to shut us down legally."

Jess let out a low whistle, her face grim. "That's a serious move," she muttered. "If they get that court order, it could stop everything — protests, meetings, even social media posts."

Michael's jaw tightened. "We need to get ahead of this," he said firmly. "We can't let them define the narrative again. We have to show that we're peaceful, that we're standing up for our rights, not causing chaos."

Mae nodded. "I agree," she said. "But we also need legal advice. If they're going to play this card, we need to be prepared. We can't let them outmaneuver us in court."

Jess perked up. "I know someone," she offered quickly. "An alum who's a lawyer. She's been active in social justice cases, and I think she'd be willing to help."

"Reach out to her," Michael said without hesitation. "We need someone on our side who knows how to fight this."

Jess nodded, already pulling out her phone. "On it," she said, moving to the side to make the call.

Mae turned to Michael, her expression serious. "We also need to rally more support," she continued. "If they're going to accuse us of inciting violence, we need statements from faculty, students, and community members who can testify to our peaceful conduct."

Michael nodded in agreement. "We'll start reaching out immediately," he said. "Letters, emails, social media — anything we can use to build a wall of support around us."

Mae felt a surge of determination. "We won't let them silence us," she said firmly. "Not when we've come this far."

Over the next few hours, Mae and Michael worked tirelessly, reaching out to every contact they had, mobilizing their network of supporters. They drafted statements, collected signatures, and organized meetings. They knew they needed to show the administration — and any judge who might hear the case — that they had strong, credible backing from across the campus and the broader community.

By early evening, Jess returned with good news. "I spoke to the lawyer," she announced as she rejoined them in the student union. "Her name is Lisa Quinn, and she's agreed to help. She wants to meet with us as soon as possible to discuss our options."

Mae felt a wave of relief. "That's great," she said. "Let's set up a meeting for tonight if she's available."

"Already done," Jess replied with a grin. "She'll meet us at her office downtown in an hour."

"Perfect," Michael said. "Let's gather our materials and head over."

Mae nodded, feeling a renewed sense of purpose. They were getting organized, building their defenses, and preparing for whatever came next. They wouldn't be caught off guard.

An hour later, Mae, Michael, and Jess found themselves in a small but tidy office downtown, waiting to meet with Lisa Quinn. The walls were lined with bookshelves filled with legal texts and framed certificates. The atmosphere was calm but serious, and Mae could feel the weight of what they were about to discuss pressing down on her shoulders.

Lisa entered the room a few moments later, a confident woman in her forties with sharp eyes and a firm handshake. "Good evening," she greeted, her tone professional but warm. "I've heard a lot about what's happening at the university. I'm glad you reached out."

"Thank you for meeting with us on such short notice," Michael said, shaking her hand. "We're worried the administration is going to try to use the courts to silence us."

Lisa nodded, gesturing for them to sit. "You're right to be concerned," she replied. "If they file for an injunction, they could potentially shut down all your activities. But there are ways to fight this."

"What do we need to do?" Mae asked, leaning forward, her eyes locked on Lisa's.

*Lisa opened a file on her desk, flipping through a few pages. "First, we need to prepare affidavits from as many witnesses as possible attesting to the peaceful nature of your protests," she explained. "Students, faculty, community members — anyone who can testify that you've been conducting yourselves lawfully and respectfully."

Mae nodded. "We've started reaching out already," she said. "We can get statements from a lot of people who were at the protests."

"Good," Lisa replied. "Next, we need to counter any claims they might make about incitement or disruption. We should gather all evidence — videos, photos, social media posts — that show the administration's actions and any signs of peaceful conduct on your part."

Jess chimed in, "We've got plenty of that. Everyone's been documenting everything, especially after the police showed up."

Lisa smiled approvingly. "Excellent," she said. "And finally, we should consider filing a counterclaim, arguing that the university's attempt to silence you is a violation of your free speech rights. If we can show that their actions are not only unjustified but also unconstitutional, we might be able to turn this around."

Mae exchanged a glance with Michael, feeling a surge of hope. "So we have a chance," she murmured.

"You do," Lisa confirmed. "But it won't be easy. The university has resources and connections. They'll fight hard, but if we're smart and strategic, we can win this."

Michael nodded, his face set with determination. "Then let's do it," he said firmly. "We're ready to fight."

Lisa smiled, her eyes gleaming with determination. "Good," she said. "Let's get to work."

The following days were a whirlwind of activity. Mae and Michael worked closely with Lisa and their network of supporters to prepare their case. They spent hours collecting evidence, drafting affidavits, and reaching out to more students and faculty for statements. The mood was tense, but there was also a sense of resolve and solidarity among their group.

As the date for the hearing approached, Mae could feel the pressure mounting. She knew they were walking a fine line — one misstep could cost them everything. But she also knew they had truth on their side, and she was determined not to let fear dictate their actions.

Two days before the hearing, they organized another rally, this time in front of the courthouse. Mae stood at the front, her voice steady and strong as she spoke to the crowd.

"We are here to stand up for our rights, to demand justice, and to speak out against intimidation," she declared, her eyes sweeping over the faces of the crowd. "We will not be silenced, and we will not back down."

The crowd erupted in cheers, their voices rising in unison. Mae felt a swell of pride and determination. This was their moment, and they would not let it slip away.

As the rally continued, Mae felt a hand on her shoulder. She turned to see Tom standing there, his face serious but supportive.

"You're doing great," he said quietly. "Just... be careful. They're still looking for any excuse to paint you as the bad guys."

Mae nodded, grateful for his words. "Thanks, Tom," she replied. "We'll be careful. But we won't be scared."

Tom smiled faintly. "I believe you," he said. "Just don't lose sight of what you're fighting for."

"We won't," Mae promised. "Not for a second."

The night before the hearing, Mae and Michael sat in his apartment, going over their preparations one last time. The room was filled with papers, files, and laptops, the atmosphere thick with focus and determination.

"Do you think we're ready?" Mae asked softly, her eyes scanning the documents in front of her.

Michael nodded, his expression serious. "As ready as we can be," he replied. "We've done everything we can. Now it's up to the judge."

Mae sighed, leaning back in her chair. "I just hope they see the truth," she murmured.

Michael reached over, taking her hand. "They will," he said firmly. "And even if they don't, we'll keep fighting. We've come too far to turn back now."

Mae smiled, feeling a rush of affection and resolve. "You're right," she whispered. "No matter what, we keep going."

He squeezed her hand, his eyes filled with confidence. "Together," he said.

"Together," Mae echoed, a small, determined smile on her lips.

The night stretched on, but they felt a quiet strength between them, a sense of purpose that steadied their nerves.

Chapter 30: The Courtroom Battle

The day of the hearing arrived with a chill in the air, the sky overcast and heavy with clouds. Mae felt the tension knotting in her stomach as she and Michael walked toward the courthouse, their hands tightly clasped together. Supporters had gathered outside, holding signs and chanting in solidarity, their faces a mix of determination and anxiety. The sight gave Mae a surge of courage, a reminder that they were not alone in this fight.

They stepped through the courthouse doors, the noise of the crowd fading behind them. The interior was cold and sterile, the echo of their footsteps bouncing off the marble floors. Mae could feel her heart pounding in her chest, her nerves fraying with each step toward the courtroom. She glanced at Michael, who gave her a reassuring smile, squeezing her hand.

"We've got this," he whispered. "We've done everything we can. Now we just need to trust the truth."

Mae nodded, taking a deep breath. "Right," she murmured, though the weight of what lay ahead made her voice sound small.

They entered the courtroom, where their lawyer, Lisa Quinn, was already waiting for them. She looked up as they approached, giving them a confident nod. "Good to see you both," she said, her tone brisk and professional. "We've got a solid case. Just stay calm and let me do the talking."

Mae nodded, feeling a bit of the tension ease from her shoulders. She took her seat next to Michael, glancing around the room. The atmosphere was tense, filled with reporters, supporters, and a few familiar faces from the administration. Dean Caldwell *sat near the front, her expression unreadable, her eyes fixed on the judge's bench.*

The judge, a stern-looking woman with sharp eyes, entered the room, and everyone rose to their feet. "Please be seated," she announced, her voice firm. "We are here today to hear arguments concerning the petition for a court order filed by the university administration, seeking to limit protests and demonstrations on campus grounds."

Mae felt a shiver run down her spine as she sat down. This was it. The moment they had been preparing for. She glanced at Michael, who gave her a small nod, and then back to Lisa, who had already risen to present their side.

"Your Honor," Lisa began, her voice clear and steady, "we are here today because the university is attempting to silence peaceful protest and suppress free speech under the guise of maintaining order. Our clients, Mae Larson and Michael Arden, have been exercising their constitutionally protected rights to free speech and peaceful assembly. We intend to show that the university's actions are not only unjustified but also a violation of these rights."

The judge nodded, her expression neutral. "Proceed," she said, her eyes shifting to the administration's lawyer, a tall man with a slicked-back haircut and an air of self-assuredness.

"Your Honor," the university's lawyer began, "the administration seeks this injunction not to suppress free speech, but to ensure the safety and security of all students and staff. The protests led by Ms. Larson and Mr. Arden have, on several occasions, resulted in significant disruptions to campus operations, and there have been concerns raised regarding potential violence."

Mae's jaw tightened, and she felt Michael's hand grip hers a little tighter. Lisa remained calm, her expression focused and controlled.

"Your Honor," Lisa interjected, "we have affidavits from numerous witnesses, including faculty, students, and community members, attesting to the peaceful nature of these protests. Furthermore, we have video and photographic evidence that clearly shows my clients encouraging peaceful behavior and cooperating with law enforcement at all times."

She handed a folder of documents to the court clerk, who passed them to the judge. The judge reviewed them briefly before looking up at the university's lawyer. "Do you have any evidence to counter these claims?" she asked.

The university's lawyer hesitated for a moment, then replied, "We have statements from campus security expressing concern over the potential for escalation. And we have video footage of an altercation involving law enforcement during one of these protests."

Lisa leaned forward. "Your Honor, that footage will show that it was the police who escalated the situation, not the protesters. And my clients immediately called for calm and peace, which the majority of the crowd adhered to."

The judge nodded thoughtfully. "I will review the evidence," she said. "But I want to make it clear that the right to protest is a fundamental one, and it will take significant proof to show that an injunction is necessary."

Mae felt a flicker of hope at the judge's words, but she knew they were far from finished. The university's lawyer continued to press their case, arguing that the protests had created an atmosphere of instability on campus and that the administration was acting in the best interests of all students.

Lisa countered with their own arguments, presenting more evidence and calling a series of witnesses to the stand — students, faculty, and community members who testified to the peaceful nature of the demonstrations and the importance of the issues being raised. Each testimony bolstered their case, showing that they were not radicals or troublemakers, but people who cared deeply about justice and fairness.

The judge listened carefully, asking pointed questions, and taking notes. Mae watched her closely, trying to read her expression, but it remained neutral, giving nothing away. She felt her heart pounding in her chest, every minute feeling like an eternity.

Finally, after several hours of arguments, the judge called for a brief recess. "We will reconvene in one hour," she announced. "I want to review the evidence presented before making any further decisions."

Mae let out a breath she hadn't realized she'd been holding. She turned to Michael, who gave her a small, encouraging smile.

"You're doing great," he whispered. "We're making our case."

"I hope it's enough," Mae replied softly. "I hope she sees the truth."

Lisa leaned over, her expression serious but calm. "We're in a good position," she said. "But don't let your guard down. They might still have a few tricks up their sleeve."

Mae nodded, feeling a mix of anxiety and determination. "We won't," she promised. "We're ready for whatever comes next."

During the recess, Mae and Michael stepped outside for some fresh air. The crowd of supporters was still gathered outside the courthouse, their faces filled with hope and concern. As soon as they saw Mae and Michael, a cheer went up, and Mae felt a surge of emotion wash over her.

"We're with you!" someone shouted. "Stay strong!"

Mae smiled, raising her hand in a gesture of gratitude. "Thank you!" she called back. "We're fighting for all of us!"

Michael put his arm around her shoulders, pulling her close. "We've got a lot of people counting on us," he murmured.

"I know," Mae replied, feeling the weight of their expectations but also the strength of their support. "We won't let them down."

As they turned to head back inside, Mae spotted a familiar face in the crowd — Tom. He gave her a small nod, his expression serious but supportive. She nodded back, feeling a quiet sense of solidarity. They were all in this together now.

Back in the courtroom, the tension was even higher. Mae took her seat, her heart pounding as the judge re-entered the room and called everyone to order. "After reviewing the evidence," the judge began, "I am inclined to allow further argument on the matter. I want to ensure that all sides have had a fair opportunity to present their cases."

The university's lawyer stood up again, his face serious. "Your Honor, we would like to present new evidence," he said. "We have a statement from an anonymous source within the student body claiming that there were plans to escalate the protests to include property damage and possible violence."

Mae felt a jolt of anger and disbelief. "That's a lie!" she whispered fiercely. "We've never planned anything like that!"

Lisa immediately stood up, her voice firm. "Your Honor, we object to the introduction of unverified and anonymous claims at this stage. This is a clear attempt to shift the narrative without any basis in fact."

The judge nodded, looking thoughtful. "I agree," she said. "Unless you have more concrete evidence, I am not inclined to consider this statement."

Mae felt a rush of relief. But the university's lawyer wasn't finished. "We also have reports of outside agitators being invited to campus events," he continued, "individuals with a history of causing disruptions."

Lisa didn't miss a beat. "Your Honor, these claims are speculative at best and irrelevant to the specific actions of my clients," she argued. "The university is grasping at straws, trying to create fear where there is none."

The judge raised a hand, signaling for silence. "Enough," she said firmly. "I have heard enough. I will now take some time to deliberate and will return with my decision."

Mae's heart pounded in her chest as the judge left the room. She felt Michael's hand grip hers tighter, grounding her. "We've done everything we could," he whispered. "Now we just have to wait."

Mae nodded, feeling a wave of nervous anticipation. "I know," she murmured, "but I'm still scared."

Michael squeezed her hand again. "Whatever happens," he said softly, "we're in this together."

"Together," Mae repeated, finding comfort in the word, in their connection.

The wait felt like an eternity. Mae sat in silence, her mind racing with possibilities. She knew they had a strong case, but she also knew how unpredictable the legal system could be. Finally, *after what felt like hours, the judge re-entered the room, her expression serious.*

"Please be seated," she announced. The room fell silent, everyone holding their breath.

"After considering all the evidence and arguments presented," the judge began, "I find that there is insufficient grounds to grant the injunction requested by the university. The protests, as they have been conducted, do not constitute a threat to public safety or university operations that would warrant such an extreme measure."

Mae felt a surge of relief so strong she almost gasped. She gripped Michael's hand tighter, her heart soaring.

"However," the judge continued, "I do caution all parties involved that any future actions that do escalate to violence or significant disruption could result in a different outcome. This ruling should not be seen as a carte blanche to disregard the rules of the university or the law."

Mae nodded, tears of relief filling her eyes. She looked at Michael, who was grinning from ear to ear, and she felt a rush of joy, of triumph.

"Thank you, Your Honor," Lisa said, her voice steady but with a hint of satisfaction. "We will continue to exercise our rights responsibly and peacefully."

The judge gave a nod and banged her gavel. "Court is adjourned."

As the room erupted into cheers and shouts of support, Mae turned to Michael, throwing her arms around him. "We did it," she whispered, her voice thick with emotion. "We actually did it."

"Yes," Michael replied, hugging her tightly. "We did."

Outside, they were greeted by the roar of the crowd, their supporters cheering and chanting in celebration. Mae felt the weight lift from her shoulders, the fear and tension melting away in the warmth of their victory.

"This is just the beginning," she called out to the crowd, her voice filled with renewed energy. "We've won this battle, but the fight for justice continues!"

The crowd erupted in another wave of cheers, their voices filling the air with hope and determination. Mae felt a surge of power, a sense of purpose that burned brighter than ever. They were making a stand, and they were being heard.

She turned to Michael, who was smiling at her with pride and love. "We're just getting started," he said softly.

Chapter 31: After the Judgment

The victory in the courtroom felt like a turning point, a moment where everything seemed possible. Mae could feel it in the air as she walked across campus the next day, the weight of the tension that had hung over them for weeks now replaced by a sense of relief and empowerment. The news of the judge's decision had spread quickly, and the mood among students and faculty was electric — a mixture of celebration and renewed determination.

Everywhere she went, people were talking about what had happened. Some students gave her nods of encouragement; others approached to thank her, their eyes bright with hope. Mae felt a warm glow of pride and gratitude. They had stood their ground, fought back, and won a significant battle. But she knew there was still a long road ahead.

When she reached the main courtyard, she saw Michael standing near the administration building, talking to a group of students. He looked up and waved her over with a grin. As Mae approached, he pulled her into a hug, his face alight with excitement.

"We did it," he said, his voice filled with joy. "We really did it."

"We did," Mae agreed, her heart swelling with emotion. "But we're not done yet. The administration won't just back down because they lost in court. They're going to try something else."

Michael nodded, his expression growing serious. "I know," he replied. "But we've shown them we won't be intimidated. And we've got more support now than ever."

"Exactly," Mae said. "We need to keep building on this momentum. Keep pushing for transparency and accountability."

"We should organize another town hall," Michael suggested. "Invite faculty, students, and community members. Make it clear that we're not just fighting against something — we're fighting for something."

Mae nodded, feeling a surge of determination. "Yes," she agreed. "Let's make it big, make it impossible for the administration to ignore."

By midday, Mae and Michael were back in action, coordinating with their supporters, reaching out to student groups, and drafting invitations for the town hall. They planned to hold it in the largest auditorium on campus and invite local media to cover the event. They knew that if they could show a united front, with support from across the university and the community, it would be harder for the administration to dismiss their demands.

As they worked, Jess joined them, her face flushed with excitement. "I've been talking to some of the faculty," she reported. "A lot of them are ready to speak out now that we've won in court. They just needed to see that we could stand up to the administration."

"That's great news," Mae said, smiling. "We need as many voices as we can get. And if we can get some of the more influential faculty members on board, it will be even harder for the administration to ignore us."

"I'll keep working on it," Jess promised. "We're getting stronger every day."

"Good," Michael replied. "And let's make sure we're prepared for whatever the administration tries next. They're going to fight back, and we need to be ready."

Mae nodded in agreement. "We've already shown we can beat them in court," she said. "Now, let's show them we can win the hearts and minds of this campus."

That evening, Mae and Michael sat together in the student union, reviewing their plans for the town hall. The room was buzzing with activity, students and faculty milling around, discussing their next moves. Mae could feel the energy building, a sense of purpose and unity that had been missing before.

"I think we should open the town hall with a speech that lays out our vision," Michael suggested. "Not just what we're against, but what we're for — a university that values transparency, fairness, and the voices of its students and faculty."

"Absolutely," Mae agreed. "We need to make it clear that this isn't just about our personal fight with the administration. It's about creating a better university for everyone."

Michael nodded. "And we should highlight the support we've received — from faculty, from alumni, from the community. Show that this is a broad movement, not just a few disgruntled students."

"I like it," Mae said, feeling a surge of excitement. "And we should also have a segment where people can share their stories — about how they've been affected by the administration's policies, how they feel about the lack of transparency and accountability."

"That's a great idea," Michael replied. "It will make it personal, real. People need to see the human side of this fight."

Mae smiled, feeling a renewed sense of purpose. "Let's do it," she said. "Let's make this town hall something they can't ignore."

The next day, they began spreading the word about the town hall, posting flyers around campus, sending emails to faculty and student groups, and reaching out to local media. The response was immediate and enthusiastic. Students were eager to participate, and several faculty members reached out, offering to speak or provide support.

Mae felt a growing sense of excitement as the day of the town hall approached. They were building something powerful, something that could bring real change. But she also knew they had to be careful. The administration would not sit by idly while they gained momentum.

Two days before the town hall, Mae received a message from an unknown number. Her heart skipped a beat as she read it.

Unknown: *Mae, it's Lisa. I just got word that the administration is planning a counter-move. They're looking for any excuse to discredit you and Michael. Be prepared. I'll keep you updated.*

Mae felt a knot form in her stomach. She quickly showed the message to Michael, who frowned, his expression darkening.

"What do you think they'll try?" he asked, his voice tense.

"I don't know," Mae replied, "but we need to be ready for anything. They're desperate, and they're going to play dirty."

Michael nodded. "Agreed. We'll need to be careful — make sure everything we do is above board, no room for them to twist it."

"Let's double-check everything," Mae suggested. "Make sure all our speakers are prepared, that our messaging is clear. And we should have people documenting everything, just in case."

"Good idea," Michael said. "And we should talk to Lisa again, see if she has any more details."

Mae nodded, feeling a mix of anxiety and resolve. They had come so far, and they couldn't let the administration derail them now. "We're ready," she said, more to herself than to Michael. "We'll face whatever they throw at us."

On the day of the town hall, the atmosphere on campus was charged with anticipation. The auditorium filled quickly, with students, faculty, community members, and even some reporters taking their seats. Mae could feel the energy in the room, a mixture of excitement, curiosity, and a bit of tension. She knew this was their chance to make their case, to show that they were serious and committed to their cause.

Michael stood beside her, his hand resting on her shoulder. "You ready?" he asked softly.

"Ready," Mae replied, taking a deep breath. "Let's do this."

They walked to the front of the auditorium, where a microphone had been set up. The room quieted as they approached, all eyes on them. Mae felt a flutter of nerves, but she pushed it down, focusing on the faces of their supporters, the people who believed in them.

"Thank you all for coming," Mae began, her voice strong and clear. "We're here today because we believe in a better future for our university — one where transparency, accountability, and fairness are not just words, but actions. We've seen what happens when power goes unchecked, when voices are silenced. And we're here to say that we will not be silenced."

The room erupted in applause, and Mae felt a surge of adrenaline. She glanced at Michael, who nodded encouragingly, and she continued.

"This fight isn't just about us," she went on. "It's about all of us — students, faculty, staff, and the entire community. We are

stronger when we stand together, when we demand the kind of university we all deserve."

More applause, louder this time. Mae felt a swell of emotion. They were being heard. They were making a difference.

"We're going to open the floor to anyone who wants to share their story," Michael added, stepping forward. "This is about all of us, and we want to hear from you. Your voices matter."

A hand shot up from the audience, followed by another and another. Mae felt a wave of warmth spread through her chest. People wanted to speak, to be a part of this movement.

The first speaker was a faculty member, a respected professor who had been at the university for over twenty years. "I've seen this administration change," she said, her voice steady but filled with emotion. "I've seen them become more secretive, more controlling. It's time for a change. I stand with you."

The audience erupted in applause again, and Mae felt tears prick at her eyes. This was what they were fighting for — a university that stood for its values, for its people.

As more people spoke, sharing their experiences and their hopes for the future, Mae felt a growing sense of solidarity and purpose. They were building something powerful, something that could bring real change.

But then, halfway through the town hall, Mae noticed a group of people in the back of the room — a small cluster of individuals in suits, whispering to one another, their expressions serious. She felt a prickle of unease. Something wasn't right.

"Michael," she whispered, nudging him. "Do you see them?"

Michael followed her gaze, his face tightening. "Yeah," he murmured. "I don't like it. They're from the administration."

"Do you think they're here to cause trouble?" Mae asked, her heart beating faster.

"Maybe," Michael replied. "Or maybe they're just here to gather information, to see how strong we really are."

"Stay alert," Mae said. "If they try to disrupt this, we need to be ready."

Michael nodded, and they continued with the town hall, keeping one eye on the group in the back. Mae felt a knot of anxiety in her stomach, but she pushed it down. They had to stay focused, stay strong. They couldn't let fear win.

As the town hall continued, the atmosphere grew more charged. More voices spoke up, more stories were shared, and the energy in the room was palpable. But Mae couldn't shake the feeling that something was about to happen, something that could change everything.

And then, just as the last speaker was finishing, one of the people in the back stood up, raising a hand. "Excuse me," he called out, his voice cutting through the room like a knife. "I have a question."

Mae felt her heart skip a beat. "Go ahead," she said, her voice steady despite the nervous flutter in her stomach.

"What gives you the right to speak for the entire student body?" the man asked, his tone sharp and confrontational. "Who elected you to represent us?"

Mae felt a surge of anger. "I'm not claiming to speak for everyone," she replied calmly. "I'm speaking for those who feel that their voices have been ignored or silenced by this administration. We're here because we believe in a better future for all of us."

"And what about the disruption you're causing?" the man continued. "The damage to the university's reputation? Do you really think that's helping anyone?"

Mae could feel the tension rising in the room, but she refused to back down. "We're here to demand accountability," she said firmly. "If the administration is worried about its reputation, maybe it should focus on being transparent and fair instead of trying to silence dissent."

The room erupted in applause again, but Mae could see the man's face tighten with frustration. She knew they were being tested, pushed to see if they would lose their composure, their focus.

Michael stepped forward, his voice calm but forceful. "This isn't about damage," he said. "It's about change. Real change that benefits everyone, not just a select few."

The man sat down, his face flushed with anger. Mae took a deep breath, feeling the support of the room behind her. They had passed another test, held their ground once more.

But she knew the fight was far from over. The administration was still looking for ways to undermine them, to discredit them. They had won a battle, but the war was still raging.

Chapter 32: Escalation and Retaliation

The town hall had been a success, a powerful demonstration of unity and resolve. But as the days passed, Mae couldn't shake the feeling that they were still walking on a knife's edge. The administration had been too quiet, too controlled. She knew they were planning something — something designed to catch them off guard.

Mae and Michael spent their days meeting with supporters, strategizing, and preparing for any new challenges. They had gained momentum, but they couldn't afford to be complacent. The administration had resources, connections, and experience on their side. They wouldn't back down easily.

One afternoon, as Mae was walking across campus, her phone buzzed in her pocket. She pulled it out and saw a message from Jess.

Jess: Urgent. Meet me at the café near the science building ASAP. We've got a problem.

Mae felt her heart skip a beat. She quickly replied and headed toward the café, her mind racing with possibilities. When she arrived, she saw Jess sitting at a corner table, her face pale and tense. Mae hurried over, sliding into the seat across from her.

"What's going on?" Mae asked, her voice tight with concern.

"I just got word from one of my contacts in the administration," Jess said, her voice low. "They're planning to issue a series of disciplinary actions against students and faculty who have been most vocal in supporting us. They're trying to divide us, scare people into silence."

Mae felt a surge of anger. "Can they do that?" she asked. "Isn't that retaliation?"

Jess nodded. "It is, but they're going to frame it as unrelated. They're going to claim it's based on previous conduct, academic performance, or other vague reasons. They're trying to make it look legitimate."

"We can't let them get away with this," Mae said, her hands clenching into fists. "We need to get ahead of this, make it clear that it's retaliation and intimidation."

"Agreed," Jess replied. "But we need to move fast. They're planning to announce it tomorrow morning."

Mae took a deep breath, her mind racing. "We need to rally our supporters," she said. "We need statements from faculty, students, anyone who can attest to the real reason behind these actions. And we need to get the media involved, make sure the public sees this for what it is."

Jess nodded. "I'll start reaching out to the contacts we have," she said. "You talk to Michael and see if he can organize a response."

"I'm on it," Mae replied. "We'll fight this, just like we've fought everything else."

Mae found Michael in the student union, talking with a group of student leaders. She quickly pulled him aside, explaining what Jess had told her. His face grew serious, his brow furrowing with concern.

"This is bad," Michael muttered. "They're trying to cut us off at the knees, make it too costly for people to keep supporting us."

"I know," Mae replied. "But if we can expose it as the retaliation it is, we can turn it back on them. Make it clear they're trying to silence dissent."

"We need a plan," Michael said. "Let's gather everyone who's been targeted and get their stories out there. Make a video, write an open letter, something that shows what's really happening."

"And we should hold another protest," Mae added. "Make it clear that we won't be intimidated. If they want to try to silence us, we'll be even louder."

Michael nodded, his face set with determination. "Okay," he said. "Let's get to work. We don't have much time."

The next morning, the administration released their announcement — a list of students and faculty who were facing disciplinary actions for various reasons, all vague and nonspecific. But Mae and Michael were ready. They had spent the night collecting statements, recording videos, and preparing their response.

As soon as the announcement went public, they launched their counter-campaign. Social media was flooded with stories from those who had been targeted, describing the real reasons behind their discipline — their vocal support for Mae and Michael's movement, their participation in protests and town halls.

Mae stood in the main courtyard with Michael, surrounded by their supporters, as they prepared for another rally. The media was there, cameras rolling, reporters jotting down notes. Mae felt a mix of anxiety and determination. They were walking into another battle, but they were ready.

"Today, we are here to stand against retaliation," Mae shouted, her voice carrying across the courtyard. "The administration thinks they can silence us with fear, but they are wrong. We will not be silenced, and we will not back down!"

The crowd cheered, their voices rising in a wave of sound. Mae felt a surge of adrenaline, a sense of purpose filling her chest.

"This is our campus," Michael added, stepping forward. "Our voices matter, our rights matter. And we will keep fighting until justice is served!"

The crowd erupted again, and Mae felt a swell of pride and determination. They were being heard, and they were not backing down.

But as the rally continued, Mae noticed something out of the corner of her eye — a group of administrators standing on the steps of the administration building, watching them closely. She felt a prickle of unease, but she refused to be intimidated.

"Stay focused," she whispered to Michael. "They're watching us, waiting for us to make a mistake."

"We won't," Michael replied, his voice steady. "We've got this."

The days that followed were a whirlwind of activity. The administration's attempt to silence them had backfired, sparking even more outrage among students and faculty. Mae and Michael continued to rally support, organizing protests, town halls, and media appearances. They were building a powerful coalition, one that was becoming harder and harder for the administration to ignore.

But Mae knew they couldn't let their guard down. The administration was desperate, and desperate people did desperate things. They needed to be ready for whatever came next.

One evening, as Mae and Michael were walking back to his apartment after another long day, Mae's phone buzzed with a new message. She glanced at the screen and saw it was from Tom.

Tom: *Meet me at the library. Now. It's important.*

Mae felt a surge of anxiety. "Tom wants to meet," she told Michael. "He says it's important."

"Do you think he's found something?" Michael asked, his face tense.

"Maybe," Mae replied. "But if he says it's important, we need to go."

Michael nodded. "Let's go," he said, his voice firm. "We need to know what he's found."

They reached the library and found Tom waiting for them in a quiet corner on the third floor. His face was pale, his expression serious.

"Tom," Mae greeted cautiously. "What's going on?"

Tom glanced around, making sure they were alone. "I've been digging," he said quietly. "And I found something. Something big."

Mae felt her heart pound in her chest. "What did you find?" she asked, her voice barely a whisper.

Tom took a deep breath. "There's a paper trail," he said. "Payments, favors, connections — all leading back to the administration. They've been using university funds for personal expenses, making deals with certain board members... it's worse than we thought."

Mae felt a surge of disbelief. "Are you serious?" she whispered. "Do you have proof?"

Tom nodded, pulling out a folder. "It's all here," he said. "Emails, bank records, internal memos. If we release this, it could blow the whole thing wide open."

Mae felt a mix of fear and excitement. "This could change everything," she murmured. "But... it's dangerous. If they find out you've been digging around..."

Tom shrugged, his face tense but resolute. "I know," he said quietly. "But I believe in what you're doing. This place needs to change, and if this can help, then it's worth the risk."

Mae felt a surge of gratitude. "Thank you," she whispered, clutching the folder tightly. "We'll use this carefully."

Tom nodded, his expression serious. "Just... be careful," he warned. "They're not going to go down without a fight."

"We will," Mae promised. "And we're ready."

Back at Michael's apartment, they spread the documents out on the table, their eyes scanning the evidence. It was damning — emails detailing questionable financial transactions, records of favors exchanged between the dean and several board members, all pointing to a pattern of corruption and misuse of university funds.

"This is it," Michael murmured, his voice filled with awe. "This is the leverage we need."

"But how do we use it?" Mae asked, her brow furrowed. "If we just leak it to the press, they'll try to discredit us. We need to present it in a way they can't refute."

Michael thought for a moment, his eyes narrowing. "What if we go public at the next board meeting?" he suggested. "Present the evidence directly to the board, force their hand. If they see this, they might realize they have no choice but to back down."

Mae nodded slowly, considering the idea. "It's risky," she said. "But it could work. We need to make sure we have enough support, enough eyes on us that they can't just sweep this under the rug."

"We'll need to gather our allies," Michael agreed. "Make sure the media is there, make sure we have enough people watching to hold them accountable."

Mae took a deep breath, feeling a mixture of fear and determination. "Let's do it," she said. "Let's bring this to light."

Chapter 33: The Confrontation

The days leading up to the board meeting were a flurry of preparation and planning. Mae and Michael knew this could be their most decisive move yet, but they also understood the risks. If they failed to present the evidence clearly and convincingly, the administration would seize any opportunity to discredit them.

Mae felt the pressure mounting as she moved through the campus, rallying support, gathering allies, and ensuring that their coalition was strong. They needed every bit of leverage they could muster — faculty, students, alumni, even sympathetic local officials. She felt a mix of nerves and excitement, knowing that they were about to face their biggest test yet.

The morning of the board meeting dawned with a sense of anticipation. Mae arrived early at the administration building, her heart pounding in her chest. Michael was already there, speaking with a group of their core supporters — Jess, Tom, a few faculty members, and some prominent student leaders. When he saw her, he gave her a reassuring smile.

"Ready?" he asked softly, his eyes filled with determination.

"Ready," Mae replied, though her stomach churned with anxiety. "We've prepared for this. We've got the evidence. Now it's time to make our case."

Michael nodded, his hand finding hers, squeezing it tightly. "We do this together," he said firmly. "No matter what."

"Together," Mae agreed, feeling a surge of strength from his touch. "Let's do this."

The board meeting was being held in a large conference room on the top floor of the administration building. Mae and Michael walked in with their group, feeling the eyes of the board members on them as they entered. The room was filled with a mix of tension and curiosity, the air heavy with anticipation.

Dean Caldwell sat at the head of the table, her expression cool and composed, her eyes sharp as she watched them take their seats. The board members were a mixture of faculty, administrative staff, and a few notable alumni, all with varied expressions ranging from skepticism to guarded interest.

"Thank you for joining us today," Dean Caldwell began, her tone formal and clipped. "We understand that you have some concerns you wish to present to the board."

Mae felt her pulse quicken. This was it. She glanced at Michael, who gave her a small nod, and then stood up, holding the folder with the documents Tom had provided.

"Thank you, Dean Caldwell, and members of the board," Mae began, her voice steady. "We're here today because we believe that our university deserves better. We've been fighting for transparency, accountability, and fairness — values that we believe should be at the core of our institution."

She took a deep breath, feeling the weight of the room pressing down on her. "But we've discovered evidence that suggests these values are not being upheld. That, in fact, there has been a pattern of financial misconduct and misuse of university funds by certain members of the administration."

There was a murmur of surprise and tension in the room. Mae could see the board members exchanging glances, their expressions ranging from disbelief to concern. Dean Caldwell's face tightened, her eyes narrowing slightly.

"And what evidence do you have of these... allegations?" Dean Caldwell asked, her voice sharp.

Michael stood up, stepping forward. "We have documents," he said, his voice clear and confident. "Emails, financial records, internal memos — all pointing to a pattern of behavior that raises serious ethical and legal concerns."

He handed a copy of the documents to the board members, and Lisa, their lawyer, stepped forward to explain the significance of each piece of evidence. "These documents show a clear misuse of university resources," she explained. "Personal expenses disguised as official costs, questionable payments to certain board members, and attempts to cover up these transactions."

The room fell silent as the board members reviewed the evidence. Mae watched their faces closely, trying to gauge their reactions. She could see a mix of shock, doubt, and growing unease.

"This is a serious accusation," one of the board members finally said, a middle-aged woman with a stern expression. "Do you have any corroborating witnesses?"

Jess, who had been standing at the back, stepped forward. "I've spoken to several faculty members who were pressured to stay silent or face retaliation," she said. "They are willing to come forward, but only if they are guaranteed protection from reprisals."

Dean Caldwell's face hardened. "These are very serious allegations," she repeated, her tone icy. "And if they prove to be unfounded, there will be consequences."

Mae felt a spark of anger. "We're not afraid of the truth," she replied, her voice firm. "And we're not afraid of consequences if it means exposing what's really happening."

The tension in the room ratcheted up another notch. The board members looked at one another, murmuring in low voices. Mae could feel the pressure building, but she refused to back down. They had come this far, and they weren't turning back now.

Finally, one of the board members, an older man with a kind face, cleared his throat. "I think it's clear that we need to investigate these claims thoroughly," he said. "We owe it to the university and to the students to ensure that our administration is acting ethically and transparently."

Dean Caldwell's eyes flashed with irritation, but she quickly masked it. "I agree," she said, her voice tight. "We will conduct a full internal review to determine the validity of these documents."

Mae felt a flicker of hope. This was a start, a crack in the administration's defenses. "We're happy to cooperate with any investigation," she said. "But we also ask for assurances that there will be no retaliation against those who come forward."

The older board member nodded. "I think that's a fair request," he said. "If we want people to speak freely, they need to know they will be protected."

Dean Caldwell pursed her lips, clearly unhappy, but she nodded. "Very well," she said. "There will be no retaliation. But this investigation will be conducted with the utmost seriousness, and if these allegations are proven false, there will be consequences."

Mae nodded, feeling a surge of determination. "We're confident in our evidence," she replied. "And we believe the truth will prevail."

The board members continued to discuss the matter, and Mae could feel the tension slowly beginning to shift. They had made their case, and now they had to wait and see what would happen next.

After the meeting, Mae and Michael stepped outside, their hearts pounding with a mixture of relief and apprehension. Their supporters were waiting for them, a crowd gathered outside the administration building, watching eagerly.

"How did it go?" Jess asked, hurrying over, her face filled with concern.

"Better than expected," Michael replied. "They're launching an internal investigation, but we've got their attention. They know we're serious."

Mae nodded. "We need to keep the pressure on," she said. "Make sure this investigation is real, not just a way to buy time."

Tom joined them, his face serious. "You did great in there," he said quietly. "But they're going to fight back. You know that, right?"

"We do," Mae replied. "But we're ready."

"We'll need to keep building support," Michael added. "Get more people involved, more eyes on this. The more people watching, the harder it will be for them to cover anything up."

Jess nodded. "I'll keep reaching out," she said. "We've got a lot of momentum now. Let's make sure we use it."

The following days were filled with a tense waiting game. The board announced their internal investigation, but Mae knew it was just the beginning. They needed to ensure the investigation was fair, thorough, and transparent. They organized more rallies, more meetings, and continued to gather evidence and testimonials.

Mae could feel the pressure building, the tension tightening around them like a vise. The administration was still trying to find a way to turn the tide, to regain control. But they had the momentum, and they weren't about to let it slip away.

One afternoon, as Mae was preparing for another rally, she received a message from Lisa.

Lisa: *Urgent. Need to meet ASAP. New development. Could be big.*

Mae felt her pulse quicken. She quickly called Michael, her voice tight with urgency.

"Lisa wants to meet," she said. "She says there's been a new development."

"I'll be right there," Michael replied. "Let's find out what's going on."

They met Lisa in a small café near campus, her face serious and focused.

"What's happened?" Mae asked, her heart pounding.

"I just received a tip," Lisa replied, her voice low. "There's someone from inside the administration — someone high up — who's willing to come forward as a whistleblower. They've got evidence that could blow this wide open."

Mae felt a surge of hope. "Who is it?" she asked. "What do they have?"

"I don't know their identity yet," Lisa said. "But they claim to have documents, emails, records that could prove everything you've been saying — and more."

Michael leaned forward, his eyes wide. "How do we get to them?" he asked.

"They want to meet," Lisa replied. "But they're scared. They know the risks. They need assurances — protection, anonymity."

Mae nodded, her mind racing. "We can work with that," she said. "We can get them protection, make sure they're safe."

"But we need to move fast," Lisa warned. "If the administration gets wind of this, they'll do everything they can to shut it down."

Chapter 34: The Whistleblower

The revelation of a potential whistleblower had injected a new sense of urgency into Mae and Michael's fight. The stakes had never been higher, and they knew they needed to act quickly. They gathered their closest allies — Jess, Tom, Lisa, and a few trusted faculty members — to discuss their next steps.

They met in a quiet corner of the library, the atmosphere thick with tension and anticipation. Mae could feel her heart racing, her mind buzzing with possibilities and risks. This could be the break they needed, but it could also be a trap.

"Okay," Lisa began, her voice low but firm. "We don't know who this whistleblower is yet, but they've indicated they have documents and information that could prove everything we've been saying — and more. We need to get to them before the administration does."

"What do they want?" Michael asked. "How do we reach them?"

"They want assurances," Lisa replied. "Protection, anonymity. They're afraid of retaliation, and they have every reason to be. If the administration finds out who they are, they'll be in serious danger."

Mae nodded. "We need to make sure they feel safe," she said. "But how do we set up a meeting without tipping anyone off?"

Lisa thought for a moment. "I can arrange a secure location," she said. "Somewhere neutral, away from campus. We'll keep the circle tight — only those who absolutely need to know."

Tom leaned forward, his expression serious. "I can help with security," he offered. "Make sure no one is watching, that the meeting goes smoothly."

"Good," Mae replied. "We can't afford any mistakes. This is too important."

Jess nodded in agreement. "And we need to keep this quiet," she said. "If word gets out, the administration will try to stop it."

"Agreed," Michael said. "Let's move quickly. We can't lose this opportunity."

They spent the next few hours making preparations. Lisa secured a location — a small, out-of-the-way café on the edge of town, owned by a friend she trusted. Tom arranged for discreet surveillance, ensuring no one would be able to follow them or interfere. Jess reached out to their most loyal supporters, letting them know to stay alert but keeping the details vague.

Mae and Michael felt the tension mounting with every passing minute. They knew they were walking into a high-risk situation, but they also knew this could be the breakthrough they needed. The whistleblower could provide the evidence that would force the administration to back down, to finally face the consequences of their actions.

As the time for the meeting approached, Mae felt a knot of anxiety tighten in her stomach. She glanced at Michael, who gave her a reassuring smile.

"We've got this," he whispered, squeezing her hand. "We've come this far. We're not turning back now."

"I know," Mae replied, taking a deep breath. "Let's do this."

The café was quiet when they arrived, the air filled with the scent of coffee and freshly baked pastries. Lisa was already there, sitting at a corner table, her eyes scanning the room. Mae and Michael joined her, their expressions tense but determined.

"Everything set?" Mae asked quietly.

Lisa nodded. "I've spoken with the whistleblower," she said. "They're nervous, but they're coming. They want to see that we're serious, that we're not going to let them hang out to dry."

Mae felt a surge of empathy. "We'll make sure they're safe," she promised. "No matter what."

Michael glanced around the room, his eyes sharp. "Where are they?" he asked. "When are they supposed to arrive?"

"Any minute now," Lisa replied, glancing at her watch. "Just stay calm. They need to see that they can trust us."

They waited in tense silence, the minutes stretching out like hours. Mae could feel her heart pounding in her chest, her nerves fraying with every second. She tried to keep her breathing steady, her mind focused.

Finally, the door to the café opened, and a figure stepped inside. Mae's breath caught in her throat as she saw a middle-aged woman with dark hair and a cautious expression, her eyes darting around the room. She was wearing a simple, dark coat and looked like she had been up all night.

Lisa stood up and gave a small wave, and the woman hesitated for a moment before making her way over to their table. She sat down, her hands trembling slightly as she clasped them in front of her.

"Thank you for coming," Lisa said gently. "We know this is a big risk for you."

The woman nodded, her eyes flicking nervously between Mae, Michael, and Lisa. "I'm taking a huge chance," she whispered, her voice barely audible. "But I've seen too much... I can't stay silent anymore."

Mae leaned forward, her voice soft but steady. "We're here to help," she said. "We'll make sure you're protected, that your identity is safe. But we need to know what you have."

The woman took a deep breath, her face filled with a mix of fear and resolve. "I work in the finance office," she began quietly. "I've seen the transactions, the documents... the payments that don't add up. I've seen emails directing funds to places they shouldn't go, favors exchanged with certain board members."

Michael's eyes widened. "Do you have copies of these documents?" he asked, his voice urgent.

The woman nodded, reaching into her bag and pulling out a thick envelope. "I've been keeping records," she said. "For months. I didn't know who to trust, but when I heard about what you were doing... I knew I had to come forward."

Mae took the envelope, her hands trembling slightly. She opened it and glanced inside — there were papers, printed emails, and what looked like bank statements. Her heart pounded with excitement and fear.

"This is incredible," she whispered. "But are you sure you're safe? Do they know you've done this?"

The woman shook her head. "I've been careful," she replied. "But they're watching everyone closely. I don't know how long I have before they figure it out."

Lisa nodded. "We can help," she said. "We can arrange protection, anonymity. But we need to move fast. Once this goes public, they'll try to retaliate."

The woman's face tightened with fear, but she nodded. "I know," she whispered. "But I'm ready. I just want the truth to come out."

Mae felt a surge of gratitude and respect. "Thank you," she said softly. "We'll make sure your voice is heard."

They spent the next few hours going over the documents, verifying their authenticity and discussing their next steps. The evidence was damning — clear proof of financial misconduct, corruption, and a pattern of behavior that implicated several high-ranking members of the administration.

Mae felt a mix of fear and exhilaration. This was it. This was what they needed to force the administration's hand, to bring the truth to light. But they had to be careful. They couldn't afford to make any mistakes.

"We need to release this strategically," Lisa said, her voice steady. "We need to make sure it gets maximum exposure, that it reaches the right people."

"We should go public at the next board meeting," Michael suggested. "With the media present. Make it impossible for them to cover this up."

Mae nodded. "And we should also reach out to allies in the media, people we trust to handle this responsibly," she added. "We need to control the narrative, make sure the story gets out before they can spin it."

Lisa agreed. "I'll handle the legal aspects," she said. "Make sure the whistleblower is protected, that they have the support they need."

Tom chimed in, "And I'll keep an eye out for any signs that the administration is preparing a counter-move. They're not going to go down without a fight."

Mae took a deep breath, feeling the weight of their plan settle over her. "This is it," she said quietly. "This is our chance to make real change."

Michael squeezed her hand. "We're ready," he said firmly. "Let's make it count."

The days leading up to the board meeting were filled with tension and anticipation. Mae and Michael worked tirelessly, coordinating with their allies, preparing their evidence, and ensuring they had the support they needed. The media began to pick up on the story, sensing that something big was about to break.

On the morning of the meeting, the campus was buzzing with rumors and speculation. Mae could feel the energy building, the sense that they were on the brink of something monumental. She felt a knot of anxiety in her stomach, but also a deep sense of resolve.

They arrived at the administration building early, their supporters gathering outside, holding signs and chanting in solidarity. The media was there too, cameras flashing, reporters asking questions. Mae felt a surge of adrenaline. This was it. The moment they had been fighting for.

They entered the boardroom, the envelope of documents clutched tightly in Mae's hand. The board members were already there, along with Dean Caldwell, who looked tense and defensive. Mae felt Michael's hand on her back, steadying her, grounding her.

"Are you ready?" he whispered.

"More than ever," Mae replied, her voice filled with determination.

The meeting began, and Mae felt the room fall silent as she stood up, the envelope in her hand. "We're here today to present new evidence," she began, her voice strong and clear. "Evidence that we believe shows a pattern of corruption, misuse of funds, and unethical behavior at the highest levels of this administration."

She opened the envelope, laying the documents on the table. "This is the truth," she said firmly. "And it's time for this university to face it."

The room was tense, filled with murmurs and whispers. Dean Caldwell's face tightened, her eyes flashing with anger.

"These are serious accusations," she said coldly. "Do you have any proof to back them up?"

Michael stepped forward. "We do," he said. "And we have a witness — someone from inside the administration who has come forward with the truth."

The room fell silent, all eyes on Mae and Michael. Mae felt her heart pounding in her chest, but she stood tall, her gaze steady.

"We're ready to present our case," she said, her voice unwavering. "And we won't stop until justice is served."

Chapter 35: The Showdown

The boardroom was thick with tension, the air almost crackling with anticipation. Mae could feel her heart pounding in her chest as she looked around the room, taking in the expressions of the board members, the administration officials, and their supporters. This was it. The moment they had been preparing for.

Michael stood by her side, his presence a steadying force. Lisa sat to her left, ready to present the legal aspects of their case. Across the table, Dean Caldwell sat with a guarded expression, her eyes cold and calculating. Mae knew this was going to be a battle — not just for the truth, but for the very soul of their university.

"Thank you for convening this special meeting," Mae began, her voice clear and strong. "We're here today because we believe that our university deserves transparency and accountability, values that have been undermined by the actions of certain members of this administration."

She paused, letting her words sink in. "Over the past few weeks, we have gathered evidence of financial misconduct, corruption, and unethical behavior. We have also been contacted by a whistleblower from within the administration who has provided us with documents that further support these claims."

Mae took a deep breath and laid out the documents on the table. The board members leaned forward, their eyes widening as they scanned the papers in front of them — emails, financial records, and internal memos detailing suspicious transactions and unauthorized expenses.

Dean Caldwell's face tightened. "These are serious accusations," she said, her voice cold. "If these documents are real, then we need to investigate. But if they are not, there will be consequences for this slander."

Michael leaned in, his expression fierce. "They are real," he said firmly. "And they paint a clear picture of how certain members of this administration have been misusing university funds and resources for personal gain."

The room fell silent. Mae could see the shock on the faces of several board members, their expressions shifting from skepticism to concern. She knew they had hit a nerve.

Lisa stood up, her voice calm but authoritative. "We are requesting a full, independent investigation," she said. "One that is not controlled by the administration but conducted by an impartial third party. We believe that this is the only way to ensure that the truth comes out and that those responsible are held accountable."

There was a murmur of agreement from some of the board members, but Dean Caldwell's face remained set in a hard line. "These documents could have been fabricated," she countered. "We need to verify their authenticity before taking any further action."

Mae felt a surge of anger. "The whistleblower is here," she said, her voice steady but filled with emotion. "They are ready to testify, to provide their own account of what they have witnessed. They have risked everything to come forward, and they deserve to be heard."

The room fell silent again, a charged stillness that seemed to stretch on forever. Finally, one of the board members, a middle-aged woman with a serious expression, spoke up. "I think we should hear from the whistleblower," she said. "If there is any *truth to these allegations, we owe it to the university to investigate thoroughly."*

Dean Caldwell's jaw clenched, but she nodded reluctantly. "Very well," she said. "Let them speak."

Mae turned toward the door, giving a small nod to the whistleblower. The middle-aged woman from the finance office entered the room, her face pale but determined. She took a deep breath, stepping forward to address the board.

"My name is Anna Richards," she began, her voice trembling slightly but gaining strength. "I have worked in the finance office for over ten years. I've seen things — irregular transactions, unauthorized payments, emails directing funds to private accounts. I've kept records, and I've brought them here today because I believe the truth needs to come out."

She held up a stack of documents, her hands shaking. "These are copies of emails, financial statements, and internal memos. They show a clear pattern of corruption, of funds being diverted for personal use, of favors being exchanged for money and influence."

There was a collective gasp in the room. Mae could see the board members shifting in their seats, their faces a mix of shock, disbelief, and growing outrage. Dean Caldwell's face darkened, her eyes flashing with anger.

"This is outrageous," she snapped. "You have no proof that these documents are genuine. This could be a coordinated attack to damage the reputation of this administration."

Lisa interjected, her voice firm. "We have already verified the authenticity of these documents with independent experts," she said. "And we are prepared to provide further evidence to support our claims."

One of the board members, an older man with a thoughtful expression, raised his hand. "I think it's clear that we need a full investigation," he said. "An independent investigation, as suggested. If these allegations are true, we must act decisively. If they are not, then we need to clear the names of those accused."

Dean Caldwell looked furious, but she seemed to realize that the tide was turning against her. "I agree," she said finally, her voice tight. "Let's have an investigation. But I warn you, if this turns out to be a baseless attack, there will be severe consequences."

Mae nodded, feeling a surge of relief and determination. "We're not afraid of the truth," she replied. "We want it to come out, whatever it may be."

The board voted to approve the independent investigation, and the meeting adjourned with a sense of tense anticipation. Mae and Michael stepped out of the boardroom, their supporters gathering around them, cheering and clapping.

"That was incredible," Jess said, her face flushed with excitement. "You really put them on the spot."

"It's not over yet," Mae replied, her voice steady. "The investigation will take time, and the administration will do everything they can to control the narrative. We need to keep the pressure on, keep fighting."

Tom nodded. "I'll keep an eye on things," he said. "Make sure they don't try anything shady."

Michael smiled, pulling Mae into a hug. "We did it," he whispered. "We got the investigation. Now, we just have to make sure it's fair."

"We will," Mae replied, her eyes filled with determination. "We've come too far to let them win now."

Over the next few days, the campus buzzed with news of the investigation. The media picked up the story, and public pressure began to mount. Students, faculty, and even some alumni voiced their support for Mae and Michael's efforts, demanding transparency and accountability.

But the administration wasn't idle. Dean Caldwell released a statement condemning the allegations as "baseless and malicious," accusing Mae, Michael, and their supporters of "attempting to destabilize the university for their own agenda."

Mae felt a wave of anger and frustration, but she refused to be discouraged. She knew they were on the right side of this fight, and they weren't backing down.

"We need to keep the momentum going," she told Michael one evening as they sat together, reviewing their next steps. "We can't let them control the narrative."

"Agreed," Michael replied. "We should hold another rally, keep the pressure on. Make it clear that we're not backing down, no matter what they say."

"And we need to keep pushing for media coverage," Mae added. "Make sure the public knows what's at stake."

Michael nodded. "Let's do it," he said. "Let's make sure they know we're not going anywhere."

The next rally was their biggest yet. Hundreds of students, faculty, and community members gathered in the main courtyard, holding signs and chanting in support of Mae and Michael's movement. The media was there in force, cameras rolling, reporters asking questions.

Mae stood at the front, her heart pounding with a mix of fear and excitement. She knew they were in a critical moment, that everything they had fought for was on the line.

"We are here today," she shouted into the microphone, *"to demand accountability, to demand transparency, and to demand that our university stands for the values it was founded on. We will not be silenced. We will not be intimidated. And we will not back down!"*

The crowd erupted in cheers, their voices filling the air with a powerful, defiant energy. Mae felt a surge of adrenaline, a sense of purpose and unity.

"We know the truth is on our side," Michael added, stepping up beside her. *"And we will keep fighting until that truth is revealed. This is our university, our future, and we won't stop until justice is served!"*

The crowd cheered again, and Mae felt a swell of pride and determination. They were being heard. They were making a difference. But she knew the fight was far from over. The investigation was just beginning, and they had to be ready for whatever came next.

Later that evening, as Mae and Michael walked back to his apartment, she felt a mix of exhaustion and exhilaration. They had achieved a major victory, but they still had a long road ahead.

"How are you feeling?" Michael asked, his arm around her shoulders.

"Tired," Mae admitted, leaning into him. *"But hopeful. I think we're finally getting somewhere."*

Michael nodded. "We are," he said softly. *"And we'll keep going, no matter what."*

Mae smiled, feeling a warm rush of affection. "Together," she whispered.

"Always," Michael replied, pulling her closer.

They walked in comfortable silence, the cool night air wrapping around them like a blanket. For the first time in weeks, Mae felt a sense of peace, a quiet confidence that they were on the right path. Whatever happened next, they would face it together.

Chapter 36: A New Beginning

The days following the board meeting were a whirlwind of activity. The independent investigation had officially begun, and the university was under intense scrutiny from the media, the public, and its own students and faculty. Mae and Michael could feel the tension on campus — a mixture of hope, anxiety, and anticipation.

They had spent hours giving interviews, attending meetings, and rallying their supporters, all while keeping a close eye on the administration's maneuvers. The pressure was mounting, but Mae felt a quiet sense of satisfaction. They had forced the university to face the truth, and now it was only a matter of time before everything came to light.

One afternoon, Mae received a message from Lisa.

Lisa: Good news. The investigators have found significant evidence supporting our claims. They're preparing a preliminary report that could be released within days. The administration is scrambling.

Mae felt a surge of excitement and relief. She quickly shared the news with Michael, who grinned widely.

"This is it," he said, his eyes bright with anticipation. "We're so close."

"I know," Mae replied, feeling a flutter of nervous energy. "But we need to stay focused. The administration will try anything to discredit us before that report comes out."

Michael nodded. "Let's keep pushing," he agreed. "We need to keep the momentum on our side."

The next few days were filled with a mix of optimism and tension. Mae and Michael continued to organize rallies, speak to the media, and coordinate with their allies. They were exhausted, but they felt a sense of purpose and determination that kept them going.

One evening, after another long day of meetings and phone calls, Mae and Michael returned to his apartment. The sun was setting, casting a warm glow through the window. Mae felt the weight of exhaustion settle over her, but also a deep sense of accomplishment.

"We're almost there," she murmured, sinking onto the couch. "I can feel it."

Michael sat down beside her, wrapping his arm around her shoulders. "You've been amazing through all of this," he said softly, his eyes filled with admiration. "I don't think I could have done it without you."

Mae smiled, leaning her head against his shoulder. "I couldn't have done it without you either," she whispered. "We've been through so much together."

Michael turned toward her, his hand gently tilting her chin up to meet his gaze. "I'm so proud of you," he murmured. "And I'm so grateful that we found each other in all of this."

Mae felt her heart swell with emotion. "Me too," she replied, her voice barely a whisper.

For a moment, they just looked at each other, the weight of their journey hanging in the air between them. Then, slowly, Michael leaned in, his lips brushing against hers. The kiss was soft at first, tentative, but then it deepened, growing more urgent, more passionate.

Mae felt a wave of desire wash over her, her body pressing closer to his. She wrapped her arms around his neck, pulling him closer, her fingers tangling in his hair. Michael's hands slid down her back, his touch sending shivers through her skin.

They kissed deeply, their breaths mingling, their bodies moving in a slow, sensual rhythm. Mae could feel the tension melting away, replaced by a warm, tingling sensation that spread through her entire being. She felt alive, connected, more in tune with him than ever before.

Michael pulled back slightly, his forehead resting against hers. "I love you," he whispered, his voice husky with emotion. "I've loved you since the moment we met."

Mae felt tears prick at the corners of her eyes. "I love you too," she whispered back, her voice breaking with emotion. "So much."

They kissed again, more deeply this time, their bodies pressing together with a new intensity. Mae felt herself falling, her heart racing, her skin tingling with anticipation.

Michael's hands moved to the hem of her shirt, slowly lifting it over her head. Mae shivered as his fingers brushed against her skin, a soft moan escaping her lips. She felt her own hands move to his shirt, tugging it off, eager to feel his skin against hers.

Their clothes fell away, piece by piece, until there was nothing between them but the warmth of their bodies. Michael's hands roamed over her skin, his touch firm and gentle, sending waves of pleasure through her. Mae felt her own hands exploring his body, tracing the lines of his muscles, feeling the heat of his skin.

They moved together, their bodies finding a rhythm, a dance of desire and need. Mae felt herself melting into him, her breath coming in short, quick gasps as the sensations built inside her. She felt Michael's lips on her neck, his hands gripping her hips, pulling her closer, deeper.

"Mae," he whispered, his voice raw with emotion. "You're everything to me."

Mae felt a rush of love and desire. "And you're everything to me," she whispered back, her voice trembling.

They moved together, faster now, their bodies pressed tightly against each other. Mae felt herself slipping over the edge, her body tensing, her breath catching in her throat as she reached for him, holding on as if he were the only thing keeping her anchored in the world.

Michael followed her over the edge, his body tensing, his grip tightening on her hips as he found his own release, a deep, satisfied groan rumbling in his chest. They held onto each other, their bodies entwined, their breaths mingling in the cool night air.

They stayed like that for a long time, wrapped in each other's arms, their bodies still humming with the aftershocks of their passion. Mae rested her head against his chest, her eyes closed, feeling a sense of peace and contentment that she hadn't felt in a long time.

"We did it," she whispered softly. "We really did it."

Michael kissed the top of her head. "We're not done yet," he replied. "But we're closer than ever."

"Together," Mae murmured, her voice filled with quiet certainty.

"Always," Michael whispered back, holding her tightly.

The next morning, Mae woke up with a sense of calm and purpose. She felt Michael's arms around her, his steady breathing a comforting rhythm. She smiled, feeling the warmth of his body against hers, and for a moment, everything felt perfect.

But she knew there was still work to do. The investigation was still ongoing, and they needed to ensure that it remained fair and impartial. She gently slipped out of bed, careful not to wake Michael, and began to get dressed, her mind already racing with plans for the day.

Michael stirred, his eyes blinking open as he reached out for her. "Hey," he murmured, his voice thick with sleep. "Where are you going?"

"Just getting started," Mae replied with a smile. "We've got a lot to do today."

Michael sat up, rubbing his eyes. "You're unstoppable," he said with a grin. "I love it."

Mae laughed, feeling a rush of affection. "And I love you," she replied. "Now, come on. We've got a university to change."

The days that followed were filled with a renewed sense of purpose. The preliminary report from the investigation was released, and it was damning. The evidence of financial misconduct, corruption, and abuse of power was clear and undeniable. The administration's attempts to discredit Mae, Michael, and their supporters fell flat, as more and more people rallied behind their cause.

Dean Caldwell and several other high-ranking officials were suspended pending further investigation, and a wave of change began to sweep through the university. Mae and Michael continued to lead their movement, pushing for reforms, demanding accountability, and working tirelessly to ensure that the values they had fought for were upheld.

They knew they still had a long road ahead, but they felt a sense of accomplishment, a sense of hope. They had faced down the forces that had tried to silence them, and they had won.

One evening, as they stood together on the steps of the administration building, looking out over a campus filled with students and faculty celebrating their victory, Mae felt a deep sense of peace.

"We did it," she said softly, her voice filled with emotion. "We really did it."

Michael nodded, wrapping his arm around her shoulders. "And this is just the beginning," he replied. "We've got so much more to do."

"I know," Mae replied, a smile spreading across her face. "But we're ready."

Michael leaned down, kissing her softly. "Together," he whispered.

"Always," Mae replied, her heart full.

They stood there, hand in hand, watching as their university — their home — began to change for the better. And they knew that whatever came next, they would face it together, with courage, determination, and love.

Don't miss out!

Visit the website below and you can sign up to receive emails whenever Summeer Fox publishes a new book. There's no charge and no obligation.

https://books2read.com/r/B-A-WOSLC-KJYZE

BOOKS 2 READ

Connecting independent readers to independent writers.